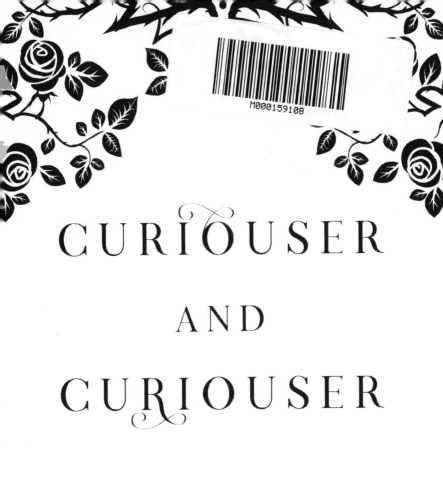

CURIOUSER

AND

CURIOUSER

STEAMPUNK ALICE IN WONDERLAND

MELANIE KARSAK

Curiouser and Curiouser

Clockpunk Press, 2017

Published by Clockpunk Press.

Book design by *Inkstain Design Studio*
Cover design by *Karri Klawiter*
Edited by *Becky Stephens Editing*
Proofread by *Rare Bird Editing*

for Semra

With love to Dana
xox

Melanie Karsak

THIS BOOK BELONGS TO:

_____

CURIOUSER

AND

CURIOUSER

1
THE POCKET WATCH

"CURIOUS." I STRAINED TO LOOK out the window of the carriage at the crowd thronging toward Hyde Park. A man on a Daedalus steam-powered buggy motored past. The well-dressed ladies in the back seat, their parasols shading them from the late afternoon sun, laughed wildly as they sped by. "Where are they all going?"

"The Crystal Palace," Lord Dodgson pronounced grandly. "The Great Exhibition opened this week. I was planning to have a look myself," he said, snapping the paper he was trying to read in an effort to straighten it, a motion he'd made ten times already since we'd left Hungerford Market. It was starting to get on my nerves.

"Her Majesty already opened the exhibit?" I asked, trying to hide the disappointment in my voice.

Lord Dodgson laughed. "Don't you keep up on the local gossip, Alice? The whole town is talking about the Crystal Palace's opening. A whole building made of glass and filled with mechanical inventions and wonders from the world afar...what a sight. I heard the opening was grand. Crowded but grand."

I frowned. I'd thought the opening was next week. The park was located close to Lord Dodgson's London home. I'd hoped to catch a glimpse of Queen Victoria but had missed my chance once again.

Half hanging out the carriage window, I strained to get a look at the festivities. The revelers had cleared a path and stood to watch as a man led a clockwork horse, its steel and copper body glinting in the sunlight, into the park. I could just make out tents sitting in Hyde Park's green space. "Then I guess that means the airship races have started," I said. In fact, the Great Exhibition's opening had been timed to the British Airship Qualifying races.

"I didn't fancy you a fan of the aether sports," Lord Dodgson said.

"I'm not. But I have a friend who adores them."

Adores, of course, was the wrong word. I tried to calm the uneasy feeling that rocked my stomach. It was Friday. If the races had opened on Monday, then Henry might already be in trouble. Had I seen him that morning? Had he gone to the shop? I tried to think back but couldn't remember. Last race season he'd gambled away everything he owned down to the clothes on his back. Even his favorite top hat had gone to some bloody airship pirate. Race season always equaled trouble for my dear friend who couldn't help but try to hedge his bets. His reasons for trying were honorable. His methods, however, were suspect.

"I'm not for any of that nonsense either," Lord Dodgson proclaimed. "Racing around the sky like we were meant to have wings. No, no. My carriage will do just fine. It gets us where we need to go, doesn't it, Alice?"

"Yes, Your Grace."

Lord Dodgson laughed. "When you use formal address, you sound trite."

I grinned. "What an odd thing to say. Shouldn't one try to adopt manners?"

"Perhaps. But perhaps not when they are completely contradictory to that person's general nature."

"But aren't manners completely contradictory to all of mankind's nature? If, in essence, we are little more than creatures who are brutish and sinful, then manners are merely a mask for the base matter that lives within us all. And if that's the case, we'd be wise to drop them entirely, if we wanted to be more honest. Or should we all lie and adopt the best of manners, thus go around being false? At least we'd all be equally false."

Lord Dodgson laughed again then removed his monocle and looked at me. "Alice Lewis, you might be the brightest girl I've ever met."

"I'll take that as a compliment, *mister*," I replied with a wink.

"Now, there's the scruffy guttersnipe I hired," he said then snapped his paper once more. "Is there another way to take that comment as anything but a compliment?"

"At least five. Possibly more."

"Alice," he said, shaking his head. He looked back at his reading.

Well, it was true. Did he mean to imply he'd met only a few women of intelligence, or that most women were unintelligent, or that he thought he would meet wittier girls in the future, or when he said I *might* be bright did that mean he was uncertain, and how did he define bright anyway? Was he referring to my hair? Or maybe my eyes? Or did he just mean he found me intelligent? Thinking about it gave me a headache, and I was already a mess of nerves worrying that Henry had already gambled away every shilling he had. Come to think of it, Bess said he hadn't been by for dinner last night.

The carriage rolled to a stop outside Lord Dodgson's home. I smoothed my white apron and grabbed the packages sitting on the seat beside me.

"Your Grace," the footman said, opening the door.

Lord Dodgson sighed heavily, folded his paper under his arm, and grabbed his cane. His bad knee would be aching after his walk through the market, but I guessed he wouldn't complain. He'd had too much fun shopping for his niece's birthday. The parcels I juggled were proof of that. I don't think there was an item left at the market suitable for a girl around the age of six. What would other six-year-old girls receive for their birthday now that *His Grace* had purchased the lot? Of course, when I was six, I'd been at the workhouse laboring on a machine until I'd found different *employment* in the city. It's amazing how quickly little fingers can learn to do very evil deeds. But young Charlotte Dodgson, the lord's niece, would never have to worry about learning how to pick a pocket. A better life was reserved for her, and I didn't begrudge her for it.

"Your Grace," the footman called, his voice full of alarm.

A moment later, Lord Dodgson cried out in pain.

I emerged from the carriage to see that he'd slipped on the cobblestone, landing on his bad knee.

I dropped the packages, cringing when I heard the telltale clatter of broken glass, then rushed to help him up.

"Steady him," I told the footman. "Easy, Your Grace. We've got you."

"Son of a bitch," Lord Dodgson muttered.

"Manners, Your Grace," I said as I gently lifted him.

Despite himself, Lord Dodgson laughed. "Ow," he said, then laughed again. "Ow...oh, Alice."

Steadying him, the footman and I helped our master stand up.

A moment later, I heard feet rushing quickly down the cobblestone toward us. The sound of it set my nerves on edge, and my old instincts kicked in. The runner didn't slow as the footsteps approached. I moved to grab the knife hidden out of sight under my apron, but my hands were all tied up with Lord Dodgson. If I let go, he would fall.

"Watch yourself, boy. What? Hey," the footman called.

A boy with a mop of striking white hair, wearing an expensive but oversized waistcoat, slipped between us and was gone again in a flash.

"My pocket watch! My grandfather's pocket watch," Lord Dodgson cried, clutching his vest where he always kept his pocket watch. "Stop that boy. He stole my pocket watch. Alice!"

I glanced up the street to see the boy dangle the pocket watch teasingly before us.

"Rabbit," I hissed.

"Your Grace…I need to—"

"Go, Alice. Go."

The footman held tightly onto Lord Dodgson so I could let go. I turned and faced the boy. Rabbit, the little albino street rat, was grinning at me. Sneaky little pickpocket. What was he doing in my part of town? He'd grabbed the watch so deftly. Not bad. Some people said he was almost as good as I used to be.

Almost.

2
CHASING RABBITS

"RABBIT," I CALLED.

The boy grinned, stuffed the pocket watch inside his coat, then turned and raced off.

"Dammit," I whispered then dashed after him.

My legs pumping hard, I pounded down the cobblestone street behind him. The boy dodged across the road, startling a horse who nearly threw his rider. If I lost Rabbit in the crowd, I'd end up having to search the entire city for him. Rabbit rushed toward the park. He moved quickly between the finely dressed gentlemen and ladies making their way toward the Crystal Palace for the exhibition.

From somewhere in the distance, I heard the boom of a cannon. An airship race was starting. I frowned again. Henry better be at his shop.

He'd promised me and Bess he was done with gambling. And he'd said he meant it. But making promises is easy when temptation is out of sight. And he'd made that promise when it wasn't racing season.

I rushed through the crowd. Rabbit was fast. If it weren't for the startled proclamations of "I say" or the tiny shrieks of fine ladies as Rabbit pushed past, I'd hardly know which way he'd gone.

The walkway emptied out into the wide, green expanse of Hyde Park. The magnificent Crystal Palace, an ornate building made of glass and wrought iron, constructed just for the Great Exhibition, shimmered like a gem in the sunlight. I'd seen it under construction but hadn't been that way since. I could see why it had earned its name. The beveled glass panes shimmered with tints of blue, pink, and yellow under the warm sunlight. Inside, I saw a dizzying display of oddities. Between me and the palace, the green space was filled with tents, vendors, revelers, and race aficionados.

I glanced upward. The first of the airships, its brightly painted balloon holding the wooden gondola aloft, was speeding overhead.

Ahead of me, I heard a shriek followed by the sound of glass shattering. I turned the corner to find a display of jars of orange marmalade shattered on the ground. The strong scent of orange peel perfumed the air. An angry-faced merchant shouted in the direction of Rabbit, shaking her fist.

I raced after him.

Rabbit rushed through another vendor tent, this one selling cupboards displaying finely painted china. I followed. The vendor was too busy yelling at Rabbit to curse me.

"Two bulls passing through," I said with a laugh at the shocked merchant who stared at us.

I turned the corner to nearly trip over one of what looked like a hundred rocking chairs in time to see Rabbit race away from the vendors toward the food stalls and makeshift taverns.

The crowd *oohed* and *ahhed* as the airships passed overhead. I heard the airship captains barking orders to their crews as the ships jockeyed for position.

I chased Rabbit down tavern row. We were in the thick of my old world, my old life. Tarts lingered, half-dressed, outside sumptuously decorated tents. The strong scents of drink and opium smoke perfumed the air. The crowd became rough and rowdy. The fine ladies wouldn't be found anywhere near here. Their gentleman, of course, darted into the opium tents, makeshift brothels, and wagering places. Typical.

I turned the last corner and lost sight of Rabbit. But it didn't matter. At the end of the row was a massive tent. The fabric door wagged. A guard stood at the door. I was in the right place. A mushroom was painted on the tent door.

I tried to quell the terrible ache that rocked my stomach. I clenched my hands, took a deep breath, then almost turned to leave.

"Anything the matter, Alice?" the guard finally asked.

I turned my attention to him. "Frog? What happened to your eye?"

I motioned to the eyepatch hiding one of his baby blues. Frog, as they'd called him due to his harsh voice—a blessing, actually, in that he'd survived a throat infection that had killed the rest of his family—grinned.

"Rough job a few months back."

I nodded. "I'd say. Sorry to hear it. I'm after Rabbit. He stole something from me."

Without another word, Frog held open the flap to the tent and motioned for me to enter.

Curious again.

3

THE CATERPILLAR

MY HEART BEAT QUICKLY. THIS was the last place I wanted to be. The tent was dark, lit only by flickering candles in colorful glass lamps from the Orient. The scents of opium and tobacco, and the tang of alcohol, filled the air. Thieves made deals in shadowed corners, tarts displayed their pert breasts to willing customers, and tinkers traded their deadly creations for illicitly-won coin. Almost nothing had changed in the year since I'd left. Except now Caterpillar was at the helm of one of London's largest crime syndicates. And therein lay my biggest problem.

I moved toward the shimmering golden curtain at the back of the tent. Rabbit was whispering in Caterpillar's ear. He nodded then waved the boy away. Rabbit slipped between the bodyguards and went to the back.

Caterpillar. Of course, that wasn't his real name. I'd known and loved him as William. But he wasn't William anymore. Now he was a peddler of opium and flesh. He was a crime lord, a dealer of dark deeds, and a man who'd broken my heart.

I hated the scene, hated that I would have to go talk to him, and hated that his blue eyes were still quick and shining. His eyes were lined with dark charcoal, ears trimmed with dangling pearls. I hated that his hair still fell over his left brow in the most charming manner and that when he smirked, one eyebrow raised. I hated that it made my stomach twist. One of the tarts offered him a glass of wine and a small bowl of what looked like dried mushrooms. He took the wine but waved the fungi away.

William drew me in. It was William who I'd loved, but it was Caterpillar who'd chosen this life over me. I needed to remember that, to keep my head on straight. I just needed the pocket watch. I'd get the pocket watch then leave.

I approached the guards cautiously, stopping just short of the entryway.

They looked from me to one another, unsure what to do.

I stared at William who toked on a hookah pipe, blowing a ring of smoke in the air.

The guards shifted uncomfortably.

William, who'd been lounging on a chaise, sat up and looked out at me through the sheer fabric.

He smirked then leaned forward. "Who are you?"

His question silenced those around him. Everyone knew who I was.

"When I woke up this morning, I was Alice."

He rose then moved closer. "But who are you now?"

"That depends. Who are you? Which Alice is here depends on your answer."

He came to the curtain. "Well then, that makes it hard to say."

"I'm sure it does, given how good you are at betraying your true nature." I was trying to keep a lid on my feelings but was failing miserably. As he drew closer, I smelled the sweet aromas of jasmine and sandalwood that always clung to him.

"You're one to talk. So, what does *Alice from this morning* want?"

I frowned at him.

"Don't get too frustrated," he replied then pulled the curtain open, beckoning me inside, "or the other Alice might peek out. Come."

I entered the semi-private enclosure. Inside, I spotted William's chief bodyguard, the Knave. A tart lay naked, asleep in an opium stupor, on a chaise nearby.

I nodded to the Knave.

"Alice," he said with a soft smile. I caught the lilt of his Irish accent in his voice. His real name, of course, was Jack. He'd been friends with William and me since we were young. As was the habit in the industry, Jack went by a pseudonym. If someone ratted you out, it was better that they had no idea what your real name might be. It's a lot harder to track a man named Knave than it was Jack O'Toole or Caterpillar than it was to find William Charleston.

"Have a seat, *Alice from this morning*," William said.

I sat on the chaise, gently pushing aside the legs of the intoxicated strumpet.

"What brings you here?" he asked, rubbing a thoughtful finger across his chin. He'd grown a short, neatly-kept beard since I saw him last. It looked very handsome.

"Rabbit stole a pocket watch from my employer. I want it back."

"What does that have to do with me?" William asked.

"Cake?" one of William's girls offered, holding out a tray on which sat a colorful selection of petit fours.

I looked down at the small treats. I could smell the aroma of the frosting, nearly taste the sweet confections in a glance. I could see the game was truly afoot. They were my favorite. I raised an eyebrow at William who smiled.

The stubborn part of me wanted to tell William, and the girl, to sod off. But the part of me who hadn't tasted strawberry frosted, vanilla-sweetened, and raspberry-and-crème-filled cake in months could say no such thing. I lifted a small cake and popped it into my mouth, feeling annoyed and enraptured all in the same moment. I closed my eyes, savoring the taste. They'd come from my favorite baker. William had remembered. Once more, angry and elated feelings swept over me.

"Drink?" the girl then offered.

I opened my eyes to see the girl was holding a bottle of absinthe.

"Alice isn't the type. Do you want some tea?" he asked.

I shook my head.

"Run off," he told the serving girl, waving her away.

The girl turned to go, but before she could leave, I reached out and grabbed just one more petit four: pistachio and chocolate. I popped it into my mouth.

"I'm glad you like them," William said, grinning at me.

The warmth of his gaze made me angry. He didn't have any right being this nice to me. "The pocket watch?" I asked after swallowing the last bite.

"*Alice from the morning* is very business-oriented. Right, then. What of it?"

"I hate it when you play coy. And you're not very good at it. Rabbit entered this tent not a moment before me. I want that watch. Must I remind you that we have an understanding? You don't tangle in my affairs, remember? It was agreed upon."

"You certainly are *Alice from this morning*," he said with a frown. "Not that the outfit didn't give it away. Crisp white apron you have there, Alice. But the blue maid's dress brings out your eyes."

"We all wear costumes, don't we, *Caterpillar* and his *Knave*?" I said, casting a glance at Jack. "Is he Jack or is he the Knave? Are you Caterpillar or are you William? Hard to tell what's truth and what's fiction, isn't it?"

William smirked then turned to Jack. "Find Rabbit."

"He shouldn't be far. You waved him off just a moment ago," I said.

Chuckling under his breath, Jack left.

"Why did you bring me here?" I asked.

"Bring you here?" William replied.

Now I was getting irritated. "Yes. Why did you bring me here?"

"Chance brings you here."

"There is no such thing. Rabbit would never steal from me or mine unless you told him to."

"Really?"

"William," I replied, a warning in my voice.

"Let's just say that a pocket watch brought you here," he said.

"For what reason?"

"Time, I suppose."

"Enough games. What do you want?" I hated feeling toyed with. Waffling between anger and heartache, I wanted to run away from the scene but couldn't.

"Ah, now there is *Alice from before*. I need that Alice's help."

"That Alice doesn't exist anymore. And why would she help you, all things considered?"

"Because of all things considered."

I looked deeply into his blue eyes. "I don't think that interests her anymore."

"Then there is nothing more for us to discuss."

"The pocket watch."

"Fine. I'll have the boy return it, and you can be on your way."

That was it? Too easy. Why did he need my help? What kind of trouble was he in? "Fine."

"If you don't mind, I'll hear another case while we wait."

"I don't care."

"Of course not. You haven't for a long time, have you?"

I glanced up at him. I caught that old look in his eye, that heartbroken man who had once loved me—whom I had once loved—but he looked away.

"And whose fault is that?"

"Yes, of course, you're right about that. It's all on me, isn't it?" he replied then turned away. "Robert, bring him in," William called to one his guards.

"Yes, sir."

"How goes the dusting, Alice? I heard you were out shopping with His Grace this morning. Must be scintillating work. Honest work, of course. Honest as they come, aren't you, Alice?" he snapped.

"What do you know about being honest or true?"

He brushed off the question. "Of course, business is busy here, not that you'd be interested. With the Crystal Palace visitors, there is a lot to manage. Hard work. So much work, in fact, that you get the impression that someone had originally intended it to be managed by two people, not one. Of course, that probably doesn't matter to you. And then there are the airship races. My coffers are filling every day. So many people just love to bid what they cannot afford."

My heart skipped a beat.

"Ah, here we go," William said. "Yet another gambler with empty pockets."

Two guards came in dragging a man between them. They dropped him on the floor. His top hat fell from his head and rolled to my feet.

I gasped. "Henry."

"Alice?" Henry whispered, turning to look up at me. His face was bloody and broken. "What are you doing amongst these mad people?"

"What am I doing here? What are you doing here?" I shot back.

"He's mad, of course. Why else would he be here?" William answered with a laugh. "We're all mad here."

I glared at William then bent to pick up the hat.

"Now, I'm afraid your hatter friend owes one of my associates a considerable amount of money. I was able to intervene, but, unfortunately, not before the good hatter got himself worked over. How much does he owe?" William asked, shooting a look to one of his henchmen.

"More than he's worth," the man replied.

Henry's suit was torn, the sleeve ripped, the shirt open. One eye was red and puffy, blood leaking from his lip.

"Henry, you didn't," I whispered.

"He did. And I'm sure *Alice from before* remembers what's done with gamblers who cannot pay," William said.

"Oh no. Not his fingers. His hands are his livelihood. He can repay the debt. His hats are in such demand that he has taken on an apprentice. He can pay the debt. I'll pay as well."

"I'm so sorry, Alice. I was just trying to—" Henry began but William cut him off.

"And how long will that take? Half a year, perhaps? My associate wants to take six fingers now. That's the standard. We can do so and be done with the matter."

"William, don't you dare," I growled.

"Alice, I'm so sorry. I wanted to raise enough money to take Bess to Bath. The winters are so hard on her. I had a tip on one of the racers—"

I raised my hand to silence Henry then turned on William. "All right. What do you want?"

"As I said, your help."

"No, Alice. Don't. You're done with that. Please. Not for me," Henry said.

"How touching. But none of your business," William told Henry. He then turned to his guards. "Throw him out."

"Alice, whatever he wants, say no," Henry pleaded.

I handed Henry his hat then turned to William. "Fine. Let's talk."

William smiled.

"Alice, I'm so sorry. This is my fault. Alice?" Henry called as they dragged him away.

"Nice chap, but he's a miserable gambler," William said.

"Poor methods, but a noble reason. He'd do anything for Bess, not something you'd understand, of course. Now, what do you want?"

"I have a problem. The situation has become…delicate. I need someone with your talents."

"I have many talents, as you mentioned. Shall I do your shopping for you? I'm also very adept at dusting, pressing clothes—"

"You know what I mean," he said, turning to pluck a date out of a bowl on the table sitting beside his chaise.

"I don't have those talents anymore."

"No?" he asked, his back turned to me. A second later, he turned and lobbed a dagger at me. The movement was quick, but something mean in me took over.

I reached out and deftly caught the blade by the handle.

I threw the knife to the ground.

"Stop it," I said.

"Stop what?" he asked, his gaze steady. "Are you still carrying her?"

"No," I lied.

"William came close to me and gently slid his hand under my apron to pull out the dagger hidden there. "I can still tell when you're lying," he said. "Of course you carry her. We never stray far from our center. I need your help, Alice. And not the *Alice from this morning*. You know who I need."

"And if I say no?" I was trembling and not with anger. I hadn't been this close to him in months, hadn't felt his touch in so long, and in that instant, I realized how terribly I missed him. The feeling confused and thrilled me.

"Then the hatter loses a few fingers."

"You wouldn't."

"Are you sure about that?"

"Yes, I am. We never stray far from our center. What's the job?"

"Nothing you can't handle." He leaned into my ear, his hot breath like a caress on my cheek, and whispered, "Welcome back, Bandersnatch."

4
THE FINE ART OF
PRETENDING TO SPEAK FRANKLY

"COME," WILLIAM SAID, LINKING HIS arm in mine. He waved
for the Knave to follow us. The sudden closeness felt very odd. Did all old
loves feel such strange inklings when their flesh touched again? We made
our way out of the tent and back into the fresh air. I was glad. The heavy
scent of tobacco and opium polluted my lungs and burned my nose.

Wordlessly, we walked between the tents and down the path toward
the green space outside the Crystal Palace. William led us to a small
arched bridge that crossed a stream. We stood at the rail, looking at
the magnificent structure. At the moment, they were holding a parade.
Circus animals—elephants, zebras, horses, and other beasts—were being
led down the promenade and into the exhibition. It would have been a

remarkable sight in and of itself, but the fact that all the creatures were made of metal and clockwork only hinted at the vast wonderland that awaited inside the exhibition.

"Take the rest of the week off. Visit the Countess tonight. She has a few odds and ends for you. Meet me before nine tomorrow."

"Why?"

"We'll be taking in the wonders," he said, motioning to the Great Exhibition.

"Whatever for?"

"Because we need to have a look."

"At?"

"At the Koh-i-Noor."

I paused, thinking back to where I'd heard the name before. "The diamond? You mean one of Victoria's crown jewels?"

"It's on display at the Crystal Palace. I fancied we'd take a look, see what kind of security is on the piece," he said with a smile. But his expression was odd. That wasn't an *I'm about to make a fortune off this heist* kind of grin.

"And what interest do you have in one of Victoria's baubles? That's a mark with an enormous amount of risk attached."

"We all have higher aspirations," he said, his voice full of false bravado. "Time to move on to bigger game."

"I can tell a raven from a writing desk," I said sharply.

William smirked. "I didn't want to ask your help, but I need that diamond. And I need someone I can depend on to do the job."

"And why do you think I'm a good choice?"

"Because if anyone can lift that diamond, it's you. And I know that you'll have my back if things go pear-shaped. Just like before."

The memory of my hands covered in blood flashed through my mind. Again, I recalled the dead man at my feet, his mouth open wide, his face frozen in the grimace of death. I closed my eyes hard, pushing the memory away. "I did that to save you. I did that because I loved you."

"Which is why I know you will help me again."

His words startled me. I opened my eyes and looked at him. A million words left unspoken flowed between us in that single glance. William looked away. I steeled my heart then stepped back. I turned to Jack who'd been standing a discreet distance away.

"Do you have the pocket watch?"

He glanced at William who nodded.

Reaching into his coat, Jack pulled out Lord Dodgson's watch and handed it to me.

I slipped it into my pocket then turned back to William.

"And where were you when I needed you?" I finally shot back. "Where were you this winter when Bess nearly died? In *your* big house, that's where. It was Henry who looked after us. Where were you?"

He opened his mouth to reply but didn't say anything. Whatever answer he might have given, it wouldn't have been enough.

I glared at William. "I'll help you…for Henry. Henry may be a mad fool, but he would do anything for my sister, risk anything, give up anything. That's what love is. Something you know nothing about," I said then turned and walked away.

"Alice," William called.

I didn't look back.

"I saved your hatter. He still has his fingers because of me."

"It's not enough," I replied, walking away. My heart thundered as I moved back into the crowd. After all this time, he'd found a way to drag me back into the mess. Why now? Why did he really want that diamond? That wasn't his style. He rarely risked so big. Something didn't make sense, and before I fell any further into the hole Rabbit dug for me, I needed to figure out what was going on.

5

SIX IMPOSSIBLE THINGS

LORD DODGSON STARED DOWN AT the pocket watch, his eyes brimming with tears of appreciation.

"Impossible. How did you manage it?" he asked with a shake of the head.

"It was nothing, sir."

He shook his head. "I owe you something special for this, dear Alice," he said, stroking his finger across the glass face of the watch. "What would you like?"

I smiled. "Might I beg your patience to ask for the rest of the week off?"

"The rest of the week off?"

"Yes, Your Grace. With pay."

He laughed. "And with pay."

"It was your grandfather's watch, wasn't it, Your Grace?"

Lord Dodgson smiled. "It was. All right. Of course. Time it is. That's what matters most, right?" he asked with a laugh, looking at the watch.

"Indeed."

"In fact, take the rest of the day off. Time is a gift best given at once."

And a gift that can't be taken back, I considered, but did not say so. "Thank you, Your Grace."

He nodded and smiled at the pocket watch.

Taking my cue to leave, I curtsied nicely then headed toward the door. Now I needed to get to Twickenham and back before dark. As it was, Bess was going to be upset once she got a look at Henry. I didn't want her worrying about me too. There was only one way to get anywhere quickly. Sighing, reluctant to bump into yet another old friend, I turned and headed toward the airship towers.

"ALICE LEWIS?" WINSTON ASKED AS he adjusted the optical devices on his goggles to look at me more closely. "What are you doing here?"

The wind blew harshly on the loading platform outside the small airship. Grabbing a handful of cloth, I held my skirt down. The ship's balloon shifted overhead in the breeze. Metal clattered gently from somewhere amongst the ropes of the rigging. Winston leaned against the rail, his pipe dangling from his mouth as he considered me. He'd grown a long mustache since I saw him last. It trailed off his chin like a walrus's tusks. Like me, Winston had left the life. Now he ran fares in his small airship. It was an honest life but not a rich one. Something I understood well.

"I just need a quick lift."

"Do you?" he said, wiping the sweat from his brow. In its wake was a smear of grease.

"Yes," I replied with a grin.

"As much as I love you, no one rides for free."

I nodded, dipped into my pocket, then tossed him two coins. "Just a quick trip. That should cover it."

"To where?"

"Twickenham."

He raised an eyebrow at me. "Twickenham?"

"Yes."

"To her?"

"Is there anything else in Twickenham?"

"Pub there serves a good kidney pie."

"I didn't know there was such a thing."

"Such a thing?"

"As good kidney pie."

Grinning, he asked, "You're not back in the life are you, Alice?"

"I hope not."

He raised a questioning eyebrow at me but didn't ask anything more.

"Rufus," he called into the gear galley. "Wake up. Quick run up the river."

"Why'd you wake me? I was dreaming of that black-eyed girl at the tavern. She was just about to—"

"Shut it. Lady passenger on board," Winston called. "And an observant one at that."

Rufus, Winston's gear galleyman, looked out. "Miss," he said with a nod. His mop of hair, twisted into a massive pile of dreadlocks, bobbed along with him. He headed below. Soon, I heard gears grind as he readied the airship for departure.

"Get comfortable," Winston said, pointing to a bench. He climbed the ropes into the balloon basket and set the flame alight. A moment later he climbed back down and unmoored the vessel. It began to lift slowly, the heat in the balloon causing the ship to rise. At the back of the airship, the propeller began to turn as Winston took the wheel and guided the airship toward the Thames. I rose and joined him, looking over the rail of the ship at the river and city streets below which grew smaller as we lifted.

"Now why would Alice Lewis be going to see the Countess?" Winston mused as he relit his pipe.

I shook my head. "I wouldn't have believed it myself if you'd asked me this morning. How many impossible things can happen each day?"

Winston laughed. "At least six."

"At least."

"Have you seen him lately?"

29

Him. There was only one person he could have been referring to. "No," I lied.

Winston grinned knowingly. "Suit yourself. And how is Bess doing?"

"The winter was very hard, but we're past it now."

"I was in love with your sister for at least a year."

I smiled. "I never knew that."

"You're not the only one who's good at keeping secrets," he said with a wink.

I stared out at the horizon as the airship glided upriver. The scent of the air blowing off the Thames filled my nose. At this height above the city, much of the foul smell died away. There was a softness to the air, and I could smell flowers and the freshness of late spring in the early May air. Each season had its own smells. Winter smelled of snow and chimney smoke, summer smelled of dust and sweat, and fall smelled of fallen leaves and the oncoming winter. But the scent of spring was always my favorite. Its sweet perfume roused my memories. Once more, I was fifteen years old, William seventeen, and we ran down the streets of London.

"THIS WAY," WILLIAM CALLED IN a harsh whisper as we raced down Westminster Bridge toward the airship platforms. Overhead, the massive aether machines moved in and out of port. The chimes on

Tinker's Tower bonged out. It was eleven thirty.

In the distance behind us, I could hear the constables' whistles, but they were following the wrong trail. William's crafty idea to throw a pack into the river had done its job. They thought we'd jumped.

Grinning, I held the box against my chest as I raced behind William. The fog on the bridge was thick, but it was filled with that same sweet spring air. Lying just under the scent of the city was the smell of new grass and flowers, of melted snow and new leaves. I breathed in the misty air. Since it was late at night, there were only a few carriages and riders passing. The fog was too dense for them to make out with any clarity two teenagers racing away from the scene of a crime.

"We're going to make it," William told me, grinning wildly.

He grabbed my hand, and we rushed forward.

When we reached the end of the bridge, I paused and put the box into my satchel. I pulled my blonde hair into a bun and pulled on my hooded cloak. William slipped on his cap, keeping it low on his brow, and we slowed to a casual pace as we moved toward the airship towers.

The place was quiet save the few airship jockeys and their crews milling about their ships. I glanced upward. The towers were nearly ten stories in height. All manner of airships were docked overhead. I eyed the ensigns on the balloons, spotting the ship I was after.

"There. The *Aphrodite*," I whispered, pointing to a ship with a swan on it.

As we approached the lift, a tower guard eyed us closely.

"You booking passage?" the gruff old man asked.

"No, sir," William replied, putting on a false Scots accent. "Just have a message for one of the captains."

"Ship?"

"The *Aphrodite*."

The guard raised an eyebrow but said nothing. He waved us into the lift. Entering behind us, he secured the doors then pulled a massive lever. The gears on the lift pulled us upward. When we reached the third level, he stopped.

"Fifth berth," he said.

We exited. Without another word, the man worked the levers once more and lowered the lift back down.

"Alice," William whispered in my ear. "How did you ever figure out how to open the chest?"

"It was a cryptix. The note we got from the buyer had a riddle in it. The answer to the riddle unlocked the cryptix."

"Riddle? What riddle?"

"How can you tell a raven from a writing desk?"

"What's the answer?"

I grinned at him. "Isn't it obvious?"

"Only to you," he replied with a laugh.

We slowed as we approached the airship, stopping at the docking ramp. There was only one lantern burning on the ship. A woman was sitting in the shadows. She was smoking rolled tobacco. The red of the ember cast orange shadows across her face, but I couldn't make out her features clearly.

"Well?" she asked.

"Are you the contac—"

"I'm her. Let's have it."

I pulled the box out of my pack.

The airship captain lowered her cap, shadowing her face. In the dim light, I could see the cap had an unusual pendant on it, but I didn't inspect it closer. Whoever she was, it was clear she didn't want to be identified. She came to the side of the ship. Reaching out, she took the package from us. She opened the lid and examined the contents. Satisfied, she closed the lid then handed me a leather pouch.

"For your boss," she said then turned back. She climbed up the rope ladder to the balloon basket where she clicked on the burner. Without another word, she unmoored her ship and started steering it out of the dock.

Wide-eyed, William watched her. He opened his mouth to question the mysterious figure, but I pinched his arm.

"Remember your manners. Never question the customers. Just do your job," I said then pulled him away before his curiosity got him in trouble.

I slid the envelope into my bag and headed toward the steps. We headed downstairs. On the second platform, William and I stopped and looked out over the Thames. It was still foggy, the gas lamps casting soft orange blobs of light in the darkness.

Overhead, the *Aphrodite* lifted out of port and flew north.

"I love this city," William whispered, staring out at the expanse. "One day, I'll be rich enough to book us passage on any airship we please. I want to see the world. Let's go to Barbados. Or to America. Or to the Orient. I want to see everything. I love the image of it. And you, Alice Lewis, I love you most of all," he said, pulling me close.

I met his eyes and reached out to touch his face. He cradled my hand in his, pressing his cheek into my touch.

He sighed contentedly, then leaned in and kissed me softly. The sensation sent chills to my toes. The kiss was soft and sweet. I caught the familiar scent of jasmine-scented soap on his skin.

When we were done, I leaned back. The kiss had made me dizzy. I saw black spots before my eyes.

We both laughed softly.

"I like your dream," I said, leaning into him. I liked it more than he knew. While my employment kept a roof over mine and my sister's head, I hated the life. The thieving, the dark deeds, didn't agree with my spirit. I couldn't wait for the day that I was released from the terrible bond that tied me to a life so unseeming.

"I'm saving every coin I make. One day, I'll be rich and powerful enough to take care of us both," William whispered.

"Why do we need to be rich and powerful?" I asked.

"Who doesn't want that?"

I was puzzled by his question. "I just want to be content. Let's move to Barbados. We'll eat tropical fruits and lie on the beach. The warm weather will clear Bess's lungs, and we'll all be perfectly happy."

"Content is easy to come by. I want something more."

"Then I'll buy you a monkey."

William laughed. "That's not what I meant."

"I know, but I have to disagree. I think content is the most difficult thing to come by. To be content is to be in perfect bliss, to have everything just as you like it. Even if you are rich and powerful, there is no guarantee you will be content."

William wrapped his arms tight around me. "Wealth and power can buy comfort. Look at Jabberwocky. He is the picture of contentment." Jabberwocky, our employer and mine and Bess's semi-adoptive father, did have many luxuries. We lived in a grand house. We had nice clothing and things. But from what I could see, he was not a happy person. He was good to me and Bess, good to his own aging mother whom Bess looked after, and when he spent time with the Countess, I saw moments of brightness in his face. But aside from that, he looked far from content to me.

I frowned. I wasn't so sure.

"I have something for you," he said. "That, I hope, will bring you toward that perfect bliss you're after, Alice Lewis."

"Something for me?"

"I spent half the job worrying I was going to drop it," he said with a laugh. "Or that if we got arrested, it would end up confiscated."

"Of course, don't worry about actually getting arrested," I said with a laugh. "You need to get your priorities straight, love."

"Love," he replied, then reached out to touch my chin again. He then reached inside his vest. From therein, he pulled out a package. "I had her made for you." He handed the package to me.

I untied the bindings on the bundle and opened it to find a dagger inside. It had a long, slim blade. The pommel was made of ivory and carved like the white queen from a chess board. But even better, she also looked quite like Queen Victoria.

"William," I whispered.

"All great thieves have a special blade."

"I love her. The queen…she looks a bit like Her Majesty."

"Such a nationalist," William said with a grin. "You'd almost believe I had it made in Victoria's image on purpose. It's a curious gift for a lady, I know. But my lady is special. She's *my* queen," he said, reaching out to touch my lower lip.

I moved the dagger aside then leaned in for a kiss once more.

"Thank you. I love her. Curious things certainly make the best gifts."

William knew me well. I didn't care for jewels or fancy baubles. I had no use for them. A dagger, however, was quite another matter. It was perfect. I slid the dagger back into the leather sheath then slipped her into the top of my boot. It took a minute to adjust to the feel of the blade, but she was secure there.

I looked up at Tinker's Tower. It was already twenty after twelve. "Jabberwocky will be expecting us. I hope he'll be pleased."

"We did just loot a crate full of cargo meant for the British Museum on behalf of his mysterious client," William said, looking upward once more in the direction which the *Aphrodite* had flown. "Alice, how can you tell a raven from a writing desk?"

Giggling, I pulled him into a kiss once more.

"That's the best answer yet," William whispered when I let him go. "Come on," he said, taking my hand. We turned and headed back into the city.

WINSTON RANG A BELL ALERTING the galleyman we'd arrived at our destination. I glanced at the small airship tower situated along the river not far from the small village of Twickenham. It was a rickety looking thing, but the port was surprisingly busy. Winston docked his ship just as another airship took off.

I took a deep breath then readied myself. Despite everything, I was, as Winston had suggested, in the mess again.

Winston looked me over, his expression pensive. "You want me to stay a bit? We can run you back."

I shook my head then set my hand on his shoulder. "Thank you, old friend. No. I'll be all right."

"I hope so," he said, nodding solemnly. "Be careful, Alice."

"Thank you."

He smiled. "Tell lovely Bess I said hello."

I grinned. "I will."

"She ever get married?"

"Not yet. But she has a fellow."

"Decent chap or should I come calling?"

I considered the question. "Decent to her. She loves him."

Winston laughed. "No luck with the Lewis girls. They're always taken. Be well, Alice."

"You too," I said, then headed down the platform. His remark puzzled me. While Bess was certainly on her way to the wedding altar, I was unattached. Well, at least I thought I was. By Winston's assessment, it seemed that the whole world knew what I could barely allow myself to admit. My heart still belonged to William.

6
THE COUNTESS

I WALKED FROM THE AIRSHIP towers to Strawberry Hill House, the little castle where the Countess lived. Lady Waldegrave was fashionable, fun, and very popular amongst the Liberal establishment. I doubted whether any of her high acquaintances, including the Prince and Princess of Wales, knew how colorful her interests actually were. Surely they must have suspected, but Lady Waldegrave, who had an appetite for exotic *everything*, always seemed to know how to make everyone feel comfortable in her presence.

The little castle was surrounded by exquisite gardens and ground, on which you could find a small guest house and a defunct building housing a printing press, all surrounded by an elaborate wrought-iron fence. No one was at the gate when I arrived, so I entered on my own accord. The little gothic castle, built by the Countess's late relative, was a hodgepodge of fashion and eccentricity. In fact, the Countess once mentioned that her late relative, Horace Walpole, had considered adding a moat before it proved too costly. As I walked down the narrow path toward the castle, I eyed the statuary in the garden. First, I encountered a rather large rooster carved from stone. It was taller than me. Around it, someone had placed painted stones of a vast array of colors. Then I noticed an arbor where roses and palm trees framed a large, shell-shaped bench. As I neared the house, ten stone goblin men lined the road, grimacing at me with angry faces.

Once I was in sight of the front door, I heard the familiar voice of the Countess. She was cursing.

"Wrench! I said wrench, dammit! You don't know a hammer from a wrench?"

"Sorry, My Lady."

When I approached the scene, I found a very distressed-looking serving girl standing at the side of a motorized vehicle. She struggled as she dug through a tool box, her brow furrowing with frustration.

"Wrench," the Countess demanded again. Her legs stuck out from under the vehicle.

The girl, so lost in her frustrated digging, didn't even notice me until I was beside her. I lifted the wrench, which had been sitting on the roof of the auto, smiled at the girl, then squatted down.

"Your wrench, Countess."

From underneath the vehicle, the stream of mumbled profanities stopped.

The Countess shimmied out from under the machine, pulled off her goggles, and looked at me.

"Alice? By the pope's knickers, I didn't think he'd talk you into it."

"He didn't. He blackmailed me."

The Countess laughed loudly then stood up, dusting off her backside. She removed her gloves and tossed them, and her goggles, into the toolbox.

"Shoo," she told the girl. "Go prepare tea for Alice and me."

"My Lady," the girl said, dropping into a curtsey. Then she headed off, looking relieved to be released from mechanic duty.

The Countess rolled her eyes. "Tell me again why you wouldn't come work for me instead of Dodgson?"

"Bess wanted to stay in London to be close to Henry. And I imagined that you'd keep company with people I'd rather not cross paths with."

"True. True. Both true. But here you are nonetheless," she said as she straightened the scarf around her neck.

I smiled at her. The Countess's hair was a wild heap of brown and silver curls tamed haphazardly into a messy bun on her head. Wisps fell around her dark brown eyes which shimmered in the late afternoon sunlight. She had the charm of someone who'd been ravishingly beautiful in her youth and hadn't forgotten it. Despite the fact that her white shirt was covered in what appeared to be oil and coal dust, she stopped a moment to tuck her shirt tail into her trousers before clapping her hands off for the final time.

"What do you think?" she asked, setting her hand on the hood.

I had seen several such autos in London. They never seemed, at least to me, to function as they ought to. Perpetually surrounded by clouds of steam or thick smoke, such tinkered machines often seemed slower than the horses they were trying to replace. The Countess's vehicle boasted brass pipework and interesting clockwork gears just under the carriage.

"Pretty," I said.

The Countess laughed then linked her arm in mine. "I know," she said. "Half the time I'm covered in so much coal dust that I look like I rolled in pepper, but I love these machines. With each new iteration, they perform better. One day, they will out-perform locomotives and put an end to the carriage. This one is special. I was able to procure some unique blueprints from a Yankee in the trade. This machine is going to be fast," she said, her eyes glimmering.

I smiled at her. Her passion made her look like she was lit up from the inside. I tried to remember when I felt so excited, so happy, about anything. "I hope it goes as you wish."

The Countess turned me toward the house. As we crossed the drive, she whistled toward the garden. A moment later, a pot-bellied pig ran toward us.

"You remember Baby, of course," she said, stopping to scratch his ears. "Where have you been, my bad Baby?"

I looked down at the pig who looked up at me expectantly.

"Go on. Give him a scratch."

I pushed down the feeling of revulsion that wanted to take over and scratched the pink pig behind his ear. His skin was hard and thick, the white hairs on his head wiry.

He snorted happily.

"Go find some truffles," she instructed Baby, scratching his ears once more before the pig trotted back toward the garden.

Waving for me to follow her, the Countess led me inside.

I'd only been inside Strawberry Hill House once before. Designed by the Countess's eccentric relative to give the air of the dark and brooding, the castle had all manner of Gothic masonry, stained glass, and gilded touches. The Countess led me to the library. It was a sunny room. The bookshelves were elaborately designed with arched peaks of a gothic design. A cheery fireplace heated the room, taking away the chill. Above the fireplace was a painting of a girl in a red dress standing in a snowy forest.

"Now, let me see," the Countess said, opening one of several parchment cases that were lying on a table at the center of the room. The long table was covered with open books, papers, gears, and all manner of tinkered devices.

I went to the bookshelf and eyed the spines. Most of the books had titles written in Latin or Greek, not that I could read Latin or Greek. I simply recognized the lettering.

"Your relative was certainly a man of letters," I commented.

I pulled a book off the shelf and opened in. Inside, I found illustrations of arcane figures.

"Old Horace? Oh yes. Lots of odd little tomes in there. He was quite interested in the occult."

"The occult?" I asked, raising an eyebrow. I slid the book back onto the shelf.

"Ah yes, here we are," the Countess said, pulling a long paper from a tube and spreading it across the desk, sending books and other contraptions rolling out of the way.

I came to stand beside the countess and looked down at the schematic.

"The Koh-i-Noor went on display on Monday," the Countess said. "I saw it myself at Victoria's opening. A rather unimpressive hunk of stone, if you ask me. I've never seen such a lackluster diamond. It's kept in a cage," she said, waving her hand across a blueprint of the display in which the diamond was housed.

"It looks like a bird cage."

The Countess nodded. "At the whisper of a touch, however, it falls into this steel box below," she said, dragging her fingertip across the design. "The pedestal is essentially a safe."

"How does it open?"

"The guards have a key for the side panel. But the diamond is lowered into the safe by a hand crank. The internal mechanism is clockwork," she said, pointing.

"All in all, then, it's just a safe."

"A highly sensitive and well-guarded one," the Countess said then leaned back. She looked at me. "What was it they used to call you? I know they love their nicknames. What was that odd moniker Jabberwocky gave you?"

"Bandersnatch."

"Ah, yes," she said with a laugh. "A girl who could snatch a soul from the jaws of death. A Bandersnatch indeed."

"Speaking of snatching. How did you come across these?" I asked, waving my hand across the schematics sitting in front of me.

"Oh, well, I do have my connections—for better or worse. Now, let's have tea," she said as she rolled the blueprint back up, slid it into the case, and handed it to me. Linking her arm in mind, she led me from the library to the drawing room.

A few minutes later, a grumpy-looking maid with a severe scowl and a tight bun entered with a tray. She eyed my dress as she poured tea for the Countess and me.

"We hiring new staff, Countess?" she asked. I'd swear I'd never heard a heavier cockney accent in all my life.

"No, Rebecca, we are not. Mind your own business."

The woman frowned heavily and looked over my clothing.

The Countess followed her gaze. "Rebecca, please go upstairs and retrieve the package on my bed. Have it loaded into the carriage," she said then turned to me. "I expect you'll be heading back soon? I'll have my carriage take you."

I nodded. "Thank you."

Looking annoyed, the serving woman left.

The Countess settled into the oversized leather chair, dropping her feet over the arm as she sipped her tea.

"So, what have you heard?" I asked.

"About the job?"

I nodded. "This is not like William. Something is off here."

She blew across her teacup. "There are rumors."

"Of?"

"That he made a deal that went bad," the Countess said. She turned and faced me, setting her cup down. "Why do you think he asked you, Alice? Why you, of all people?"

"He needs someone very good."

"You're good, there is no doubt, but do you think that's the only reason?"

I sipped my tea and didn't look at her.

"He trusts you, Alice. And he's in trouble. The deal was with the Queen of Hearts."

I set my cup down and stared at her. I knew it. From the moment he uttered the name of the diamond, I had sensed the danger. Only the Queen of Hearts would have the audacity to steal from the crown. "What was the deal? Do you know what happened?"

She shook her head. "All I've heard was that she hired him for a job and it went bad. She wanted blood but settled for a diamond."

"I don't like this."

"I don't know what the deal was, what she has over William, but if I were you, I'd find out."

I shook my head. "I don't like the idea of stealing from Queen Victoria. It's just…it's just not patriotic. And more, if something goes wrong—"

"You'll pay the price for him, and Bess will pay the price for you."

I nodded.

"I'm sorry he dragged you into this, Alice. You've been out of the job for a year, haven't you? I was surprised when he told me he was going to ask your help."

"That makes two of us."

"Well, surprised and not surprised, to be honest. Men often make excuses to find their way back home," she said with a soft smile. "Now, do you still have that knife of yours?"

I paused a moment as I thought about her words, but set such thoughts aside for the moment. I moved my apron aside to show the hilt of the blade.

The Countess held out her hand.

I pulled the blade from my belt and laid it in her palm.

"The White Queen, isn't that what you call her?" she asked, looking at the carving.

I nodded.

"Fitting," the Countess said. Then she did something unexpected. Muttering something just under her breath, she ran her index finger down the flat of the blade. Her words were too low to be understood and they were also in Latin. For a second, the blade flashed with glowing blue light. The appearance of words seemed to be etched on the blade, glowing in gold. A moment later, both the light and the words dissipated. I raised an eyebrow at the Countess.

"There. That should do it."

"I thought you said Uncle Horace was the one interested in the occult."

"Well," the Countess said with a smile. "It never hurts to pick up things here and there." The Countess rose. It was time to go.

Standing, I followed her lead.

"If there is anything else I can do for you, please don't hesitate to contact me. Be safe, Alice."

"Thank you."

She smiled. "It's the least I can do. Your former employer was very dear to me, and I know you stayed loyal to the very end, whether you wanted to be or not. You were, in truth, like a daughter to him. And he, in truth, was someone very dear to me. In an odd way, that creates a bond between us, wouldn't you say?"

It was true that Lady Waldegrave and Jabberwocky had been lovers. While her words moved me, they also struck me with guilt. Jabberwocky had been like a father to me. And I had stayed true to him. Until he was gone. "He was like a father to me. I wish I could have been...have done more with his legacy. It's just, the life wasn't—"

"No. It was never right for you. He couldn't see it. Just because you could do the job didn't mean you should. Not then. And not now," she said, her expression serious. "I don't like that you're involved in this disaster. Please, be careful. Now let's get you home to Bess before she worries herself sick," she said, handing the blade back to me.

I took the knife from her hand. When I gripped the dagger, it felt oddly cool. The Countess was an odd woman, who lived in an odd house, full of odd books, procured from her odd ancestor. And now, my blade too took on an oddness. And I knew, just from the touch, that my dagger was deadlier than ever.

"I think I owe you a thank you."

She laughed. "You do. And you must repay me. Talk Bess and Henry into moving to Twickenham. Come work for me. I need someone with a quick mind. And you look dreadful in that stupid uniform."

I laughed.

With that, the Countess led me back outside where a carriage waited. Sitting inside the carriage was a box.

"What's this?" I asked.

The Countess smiled. "A dress, a proper ladies' dress. You cannot go the Great Exhibition dressed like that," she said, frowning at my outfit once more.

"I'm beginning to believe everyone hates this uniform," I said, looking down at my white apron and blue gown. "And here I thought it was suited to me," I said with a smile.

The Countess grinned. "Good luck."

"Thank you for everything."

She nodded.

Once I was settled inside the carriage, the Countess waved to the driver. Before we pulled away, however, she left me with one last piece of advice.

"Alice," the Countess called. "Watch your head."

7
LITTLE WHITE LIES

"OH, THANK GOODNESS," BESS EXCLAIMED the moment I opened the door. She pulled me inside then took my face in her hands. "Alice, are you all right? I've been so worried. This has been an awful, awful day. Are you okay? Where have you been?" Her large blue eyes looked even wider in all the excitement. And her soft yellow curls, pale in color almost to white, hung in wild wisps about her face. The red blotches on her face told me she'd been crying.

I looked around at the small flat my sister and I shared above the dressmaker's shop. The place smelled of freshly baked bread. Henry was sitting in a chair by the window, a washcloth pressed against his cheek.

"I...Lord Dodgson had me run a late errand to pick up a gift for his niece."

Bess sighed then pushed the door closed behind me. "I don't know why he always asks you to do everything. Alice, look at Henry," she said, setting her hands on her hips.

I turned to Henry who, it seemed, wanted to look at anything other than me. He wouldn't meet my eyes.

"Henry," I said carefully.

"Beat up on the way home from work. And he didn't even have a pence in his pocket to steal anyway. My poor sweet dear," Bess said, leaving me to go to Henry. She took the cloth from his hand and touched it to his bruised cheek. She set a soft kiss on his forehead.

Henry took her hand and kissed it gently, pressing the back of her hand to his cheek as he closed his eyes.

"Sweet hatter," she said, leaning in to pull him into an embrace, cradling his head against her stomach.

The sight of it was so sweet, so full of love, that I looked away. I pretended to be distracted by Bess's cat who wove through my feet, rubbing her head on my legs. My heart twisted.

"Hello, Dinah," I choked out, pressing my emotions down. I stooped to pet her.

"Well," Bess said as she pushed her wild curls behind her ears, "now that I have both of you at home, let's eat. Oh, Alice, you really did give me a fright after what happened to Henry."

"I'm so sorry, Bess." I set the packages the Countess had given me on my small cot then went to join Henry, who'd moved to our small kitchen table, while Bess ladled soup into our bowls.

"Are you all right?" I asked Henry. A forlorn expression on his face, he looked up at me. His golden, hazel-colored eyes spoke volumes. I could see from his expression how truly sorry and ashamed he was. I didn't have the heart to be angry with him.

"I'll recover. And you? Are you all right?"

I nodded.

"The world just gets worse and worse every day, I'd swear," Bess said. "And I'd thought we'd left that life behind."

I shot a hard glance at Henry.

Ashamed, he looked away.

"Let's talk about something cheerful. Alice, tell me about your day. Henry has had nothing but bad news. I won't sleep the whole night unless I hear something to cheer my spirit," Bess said as she set down the bowls in front of us.

I tapped my spoon on the side of the bowl, then smiled at my sister. "I saw the Crystal Palace today."

"Oh! I heard some talk about it when I dropped off a vase at Mrs. Whitaker's this morning."

"Bess? You went out?" Henry asked.

"Just to drop off the vase."

"But the air was quite cool this morning. Please, let Alice and me deliver your work."

Bess waved her hand at him. "Henry—"

"Bess, please stay inside until it's truly warm," Henry said.

"Fine, fine," Bess said dismissively then turned once more to me. "Tell me, what does it look like?"

"I didn't go in, but from what I could see, it looked like…like a world inside a raindrop."

Bess smiled wistfully as she sat back in her seat. "You have such a way with words, Alice. Such images," she said then turned to Henry. "She used to tell me fabulous stories when we were children."

Henry smiled.

"Nonsense tales," I said with a grin.

"Certainly the tale of the lobster ball, attended by a snails, fish, and turtles, all lorded over by King Gryphon, was very fanciful. But what an imagination. I think many children would like to hear such stories."

"You flatter me."

"Just as much as you deserve. But no more than that. Wouldn't want you getting an ego," she said jokingly with a quick laugh, but when she did so, she began to cough. Soon it took over her. Her who body rattled as she hacked. Henry rose quickly to grab her some water while I grabbed her syrup from the counter. Bess coughed hard into her handkerchief. When her coughs finally subsided, she took the cup from Henry and sipped it while I poured her a dose of the draft. I couldn't help but notice as she set the handkerchief in her lap that there was blood on it.

"The winter cough is still lingering," she whispered between sips.

Henry and I exchanged worried glances but said nothing.

"Here," I said, offering her a dose of the medicine which she took without hesitation.

When I went to put the little amber bottle away, I eyed the liquid inside. Hadn't the bottle been full last week? It was almost empty. I'd need to stop by the apothecary.

"Do you want tea?" Henry asked her.

Bess shook her head. "No, no, the soup will help. Sit, sit, both of you. Please. I'm all right. Don't make a fuss. Now, Alice, tell us what else you saw."

"A parade of mechanical creatures. Elephants, horses, lions, all made of metal and clockwork," I said with a smile. "Lord Dodgson is planning a visit this week. He mentioned that he might take me along," I lied. There was no way I could visit such a place and not tell my sister about it. But I did not want to tell her I was planning to go with William. Nor did I want her to know I was not planning to be at work the rest of the week. I felt tremendously guilty.

"How wonderful that would be," Bess said wistfully. "He should take you. He drags you about everywhere else. Today at the shop they were talking about the Chinese vases on display at the exhibit. Mrs. Whittaker says we're likely to get a million orders for them. If you go, try to bring me a pamphlet. I'll hardly know what to paint without having a look myself."

"I will certainly try," I told her, feeling wretched that I would see such beautiful things with ill-intent in my heart when a creature like my lovely sister could not afford the luxury of a ticket to visit the Crystal Palace.

"Oh, and look at this," Bess said, getting up from her seat. She went over to the drying stand where her china cups, platters, and vases all sat. "What do you think?" she asked, handing a delicate teacup to me. Painted thereon were images of large tropical flowers.

"Beautiful," I said, eyeing the ruby, brilliant pink, and sunset orange blossoms.

"A woman brought in a book with paintings of the flowers that grow in Bermuda. Can you believe that? Her husband owns a plantation there or some such thing. She wants a full set decorated with these flowers."

I smiled. "Lovely work, Bess."

"She asked Mrs. Whittaker for me specifically. Isn't that a pip?"

"Your hands carry their sweetness," Henry said.

"As do yours, love," she replied, tousling his hair. "And what did you make at the millinery today, dear Henry?"

"A mess," he replied, pulling off a hunk of bread which he handed to me.

At that, I laughed.

Bess smiled. "That is certain. Sometimes I think your flat is carpeted with ribbons, feathers, buttons, and silk. I don't recall ever actually seeing the wood floor before. But tell me, did you make anything new?"

Henry smiled, but I noticed that his cracked lip pained him. "This morning, before tea, three sisters came to see me to ask for new hats. They wanted their monograms sewn onto the front."

Bess laughed. "Indeed?"

"They're triplets. They look alike, all three of them. Their names were Elsie, Lacie, and Tillie. They wanted the monograms so their mother could tell them apart."

Bess grinned. "What a terrible mother she must be if she cannot differentiate between her own daughters."

"Well, they do all look the same."

"But to their mother, if she knows them well, then they should not. Do you remember those twins, Devon and David?" Bess asked me. "The ones at the mill. The boys did look the same, but once you knew their nature, they were no more alike than Alice and me."

"Perhaps their mother is not as bright as you," I suggested.

Bess winked at me.

"I wrote up their order, but then it came to the issue of payment."

"What was the matter?" Bess asked.

"They wanted to pay me in molasses."

"Molasses?" Bess asked, looking puzzled. She broke into laughter which made Henry and me both smile. "Why?"

"I don't know," Henry answered, "I was about to ask that very question when one of them got the idea then that instead of hats they should order clothing from the dollmaker for their pet dormouse. So, off they went.

"Molasses?" Bess asked again with a laugh.

"Indeed. What a mad world, isn't it?" he said, looking up at me, his eyes full of apology.

I lifted my mug. "Indeed it is. Shall we have a toast then?"

"A toast?" Bess asked.

"To mad things?" I offered.

Bess nodded. "Indeed, to mad things!"

"To mad things!"

8

THE QUEEN OF HEARTS

AS WAS HIS CUSTOM, HENRY lingered after dinner for a while. As his flat was right across from ours, there was no need to rush off. And, of course, he wanted to spend as much time with Bess as possible. Once it got very late, however, he bid us farewell.

I tried not to listen as Bess and Henry said their goodbyes at the door. The soft sound of their kisses met my ears. Sliding the Countess's packages aside, I lay down on my cot and stared at the wall.

I hadn't trusted my heart to anyone since William. I had loved, and it had cost me dearly. When I left the life, I'd gone into service with Lord Dodgson and moved me and Bess into the flat to escape. That was how Henry and Bess had met. I was glad we'd gone, that Bess was away from it all, and that fortune had blessed her with love in such a serendipitous fashion, but it had come at a price.

The Countess was right. Jabberwocky had loved Bess and me like we were his own daughters. We were supposed to inherit his big house. And I was supposed to be his successor, to run the business, with William at my side, after Jabberwocky was gone. The problem was that I had no interest in the job. It wasn't as if Jabberwocky's deeds were bloody. Consorting with airship pirates to make quick coin at gaming or selling opium wasn't the same as the bloody business with which the Queen of Hearts meddled. But I didn't want the life. And it was consorting with monsters like the Queen of Hearts that made me want to get away.

To say I'd never forget the first time I met her would be an understatement. Sometimes we encounter such scenes that they sear themselves into your memory. Such as it was the first time I encountered the Queen of Hearts. It had started as a simple job, but I should have known from Jabberwocky's manner that it would be anything but.

"GO TO THE MUSHROOM," JABBERWOCKY had told me. He ran his hand over his hair, which had now paled from blond to white. It was combed in smooth rows. "Meet William. I have a package that needs to be delivered," he'd said, but he hadn't met my eye.

"Package?" I asked, fingering the small treasures on Jabberwocky's desk: clay statues Bess had made for him, a framed miniature of his wife who'd died young in childbirth, and a poem I'd once written for him that he'd framed.

"A girl. Anna. She's being transferred."

"To whom?" I asked, surprised that I'd been brought in to handle a matter involving one of the brothel girls. Jabberwocky usually kept me as far as possible from the trade.

"To the Queen of Hearts," Jabberwocky had said, passing me a slip of paper. "My carriage will take you to meet them. Go now."

I stared at him, noting very plainly how he was looking at everything except me. His brow was furrowed, and he tapped his pen nervously. It was very clear that he didn't want me to ask questions.

"Yes...yes, sir," I said then headed toward the door.

"Alice?" he called just before I left.

"Yes?"

"The Queen of Hearts's guards will check you for weapons. Take something they can't find."

"Yes, sir."

With that, I headed upstairs and quickly changed. It was early morning. Bess was still asleep. No doubt she'd have a long day ahead of her looking after Madame Mock, Jabberwocky's mother to whom Bess was a companion. Slipping on a pair of brown leather pants and a white shirt, I then pulled on a halter leather corset that was reinforced with tempered metal that could withstand a puncture. Over that, I pulled on a dark blue jacket with a bustle at the back. I left the White Queen behind, substituting her for a flat dagger that I called Button given its deceptive pommel. I slipped it into a discreet fold in the corset. I pulled on my leather boots. Inside were small lock pick pins and flat blades that were handy in a pinch. Lastly, I pulled my hair into a bun. I slipped the smallest of blades, disguised as a hairpin with a dragonfly top, into my mass of hair.

Jabberwocky's expression told me this wasn't a usual job. Rumors abounded about the Queen of Hearts. Some claimed she was in league with the devil. Others said she trafficked with assassins. There was no certainty about what her trade was, but I knew that even scoundrels like Jabberwocky generally steered clear of her. That was a good enough reason for me to stay away.

I headed outside and climbed into the carriage. The driver took me from Jabberwocky's house to The Mushroom. The pub, of course, was a front for the crime syndicate Jabberwocky ran. William was waiting outside with Anna.

"Alice," William said, opening the door and motioning for Anna to step inside.

I nodded to him then eyed the girl over. She was wearing a straw hat and a bright yellow dress. "Good morning," she said happily.

I smiled at her but knew my expression betrayed my apprehension. Anna, who didn't know me well, thought little of it. William, on the other hand, nodded to me. His expression was dark as well.

William and Anna got into the carriage, and we headed out.

"Do you know anything about my new employer?" Anna asked me.

"Not much," I replied.

Anna nodded. "The city smells horrible," she said, crinkling up her nose. "I don't think I'll ever get used to it."

"You're new to London?"

She nodded. "I came here looking for…work."

I nodded.

"At certain times of the year, the fog holds the smog from the factories and the waste dumped into the river," William replied absently.

"Did you grow up here?" Anna asked William.

"Yes."

"And your family? Are they still here as well?"

He shook his head. "Jabberwocky is my only family. I was orphaned as a boy."

"Your father is very good to everyone," she said then, turning to me.

"My father?"

"Mister Jabberwocky."

William smirked.

"Thank you," I said, not wanting to bother to explain to her that Jabberwocky was no more my father than William's. Bess and I just had the fortune of being in the right place at the right time which had landed us in Jabberwocky's circle.

The carriage took us just outside of London to the Queen of Hearts's magnificent grounds at Darkfen Abbey. The driver spoke in low tones to the guards at the gate. Wordlessly, they inspected the carriage then sent us toward the house.

The road wound through a dense forest. The tall trees, heavy with new leaves, cast a canopy over us. The air chilled, the sun blocked. The grounds may have once been beautiful, but were now unkempt. Bramble and thorny vines choked the forest floor. There was the scent of mud and algae in the air.

The medieval abbey sat on a small rise. Its roof, like jagged fingers, reached into the sky. It was made of dark stone, and much of the original stained glass appeared to be intact. The ruby, sapphire, and golden colors of the glass twinkled in the sunlight. Angry gargoyles glared down at us like stony watchmen, sticking their forked tongues out at us in warning.

I heard Anna suck in a breath, but she said nothing.

When we reached the front door, a man wearing dark robes and a black silk turban decorated with sparkling gems waited for us. He had a long black beard and mustache. He reminded me of one of the spice peddlers that often flew in from Malta. He wore a massive curved blade at his side.

"Weapons? he asked the moment we stepped out of the carriage.

"We were instructed to leave them behind," I replied.

The guard motioned to me anyway. Clearly, he didn't take me at my word.

Lifting my arms, I let him part me down. I saw William grit his teeth as the man's arms moved quickly around my breasts.

He nodded then turned to William, who reluctantly assented.

The man raised an eyebrow at Anna, giving her a quick once-over, then turned back toward the front door, motioning for us to follow him.

Once inside the abbey, the door firmly closed behind us, and everything grew dim. The stained glass above the front door cast colored light on the floor. Aside from that, only a few lamps were lit and the windows were shuttered. It was dark, dank, and cool inside. The furnishings were sparse but rich. Exquisite paintings, tapestries, and statuaries filled the dark halls.

We passed a maid dusting. I hardly paid her any mind, save to notice how very pale she looked, when she turned and looked at me. Her eyes were not made of flesh and blood but clockworks and optics. Strange wires protruded from her temples—from inside her very head—and back inside her ears. The mechanisms inside those strange golden eyes seemed to focus. She regarded me, then with a sharp jolt, she turned back to her work. A mechanical click sounded from her as she moved. I tried not to stare but couldn't look away. She was neither machine nor human.

"This way," the man said, scowling at me.

"Did you see that?" I whispered to William.

He nodded. "I don't like this."

"Me either," I said but pushed my shoulders back, steeling my nerve.

It almost worked but then Anna slipped her soft hand into mine. It was icy cold. She looked at me, her blue eyes wide with fear.

I squeezed her hand, trying to reassure her, but the confidence I felt—and tried to pass to her—was a lie. Something was very wrong here.

The man led us down a dark hallway and then another. There was a strange smell in the air, a sort of mix of lemon and decay. It made my gorge rise. At last, we reached a heavy old door at the end of a dark hallway.

The guard knocked on the door.

"Yes? What do you want?" a harsh female voice demanded.

The man motioned for us to stay put then went inside.

I passed William a concerned glance.

"We do the job, then we leave, just like always," he whispered so Anna could not hear.

I nodded.

"Fine, fine. Let's see, then. Send them in," the rough female voice shouted on the other side of the door.

The man returned and motioned for us to enter.

Even before the view unfolded before us, the smell of death wafted toward us. It was a strange scent. I could smell bodies, and feces, and decay, and also, quite in contrast, the scent of lemon and the heady smell of burnt sage.

The room bespoke itself. Mangled bodies hung on racks, in cages, and a heap of headless corpses lay in one pile. Every corpse seemed to be missing its head. But they hadn't gone far. Some sat in jars filled with unidentifiable liquids. Others sat on a workbench, being fastened with the same clockwork devices I had seen on the maid. Piles of pulpy red sinew and gears and tools lay on the table in a confused jumble.

Anna suppressed a squeal and stepped back toward the door. The main in the turban took her by the arm.

And then my eyes fell on her.

The Queen of Hearts wore a long dark red dress covered with a black leather apron. She stood at a long table cleaning a series of instruments, each looking more deadly and pain-inducing than the last. She had very pale skin. It was so white that I had to look twice to determine it was not cream giving her such a white pallor. Her skin was smooth and without any blemish. She looked like she'd been carved out of porcelain. Her eyes were so dark brown they almost appeared black. She stood looking at us as she set the last instrument down and then, with a wet cloth, she wiped off the last of the blood that stained her arms from her elbows to her fingertips.

"I hope you aren't the girl Jabberwocky sent. No offense, but you're not my type, darling," she said to me.

I opened my mouth to speak when William said, "This is Anna." He motioned to her.

Anna had turned whiter than the Queen herself. She looked like she was about to faint. Her eyes bulged as she stared at the mangled bodies.

The Queen of Hearts set down her cloth and crossed the room to look at Anna, pulling off her apron as she did so. The Queen disgusted me and intrigued me all at once. I glanced around the room at the leavings of her…experiments. What the poor souls had suffered here was beyond my comprehension. Despite the revulsion I felt, I couldn't help but realize that the Queen was probably the most beautiful woman I had ever seen.

She looked Anna over. "Why, you look positively petrified. Come, girl, this fate isn't for you," she said, casting her hand toward the pile of corpses and row of heads. "Provided Jabberwocky has kept up his end of the bargain."

I set my hand on my corset just near Button, the slim blade I'd hidden there.

The Queen of Hearts reached out and gently felt Anna's breasts. "Are you a virgin?" she whispered.

Anna looked startled. "Yes. Yes, ma'am."

"Why are you in London?"

"My family needs money. I came to Mister Jabberwocky's brothel looking for work. I know I have a pretty face. I hoped I could fetch a good price."

"Keen on getting something between your legs?"

"No, ma'am. I just…my family is in a sorry condition. We are six daughters. I just…it was a last resort."

"Check her," she told the man in the turban who nodded then took Anna by the arm and led her into an adjoining chamber.

I didn't dare meet Anna's eye. I didn't want to see the request for help that I knew would be there. I didn't trust myself not to intervene when everything inside me was screaming at me to save this girl from whatever fate had in store for her.

Unsure what to do, I bit the inside of my cheek and kept my eyes trained on the floor. The Queen of Hearts went back to the table and fingered through her instruments. She hummed as she worked. Out of the corner of my eye, I watched her inspect the instruments then set them back down.

"No gawking and no questions. I like the two of you," the Queen of Hearts said finally.

When I looked up again, I saw that she was studying us both closely.

"What's your name?" she asked me.

"Alice."

"Alice," she mused. "Oh, I see. Bandersnatch, correct?" she asked, lifting an eyebrow.

"Yes."

She grinned. "And you?" she asked, turning to William.

"They call me Caterpillar."

"Jabberwocky's opium peddler? I understand you had a fresh shipment come in on the *Burning Rook* yesterday. Be a good boy and have some sent over for my personal use."

William nodded, but I could tell by the expression on his face that he wanted nothing further to do with her.

The man returned several moments later with Anna who looked decidedly disheveled, her cheeks red.

"Well?" the Queen of Hearts asked.

The man nodded. "She is intact."

The Queen of Hearts crossed the room and took Anna by the arm.

"Now, one more check, my dear," the Queen of Hearts told Anna then sat her down in a chair at the end of the row of instruments. The girl's face was alive with fear. It was all I could do to keep myself from grabbing Anna and rushing out of there. I reminded myself over and over again that Anna had chosen to sell herself. She had chosen this life. She had come by her own free will. Who was I to intervene?

The Queen of Hearts took Anna's arm and gently extended it. "Don't be afraid. This last test will ensure that you'll be of use to me. If not, I'll send you back with these two. If so, you'll be paid handsomely for your... goods, and no meat will ever pass between those legs," she said, and then patted the girl on her cheek. "At least until the bloom fades."

She then pulled a tight leather strap around Anna's forearm. The girl winced with pain, but I could see she was trying to be brave.

The Queen lifted a syringe with an attached tube from the table. She motioned for her man to help. He picked up a silver bowl and held it, aiming the tube toward the bowl.

Moving carefully, the Queen inspected Anna's arm then smiled at her.

"This will prick a little, but less than a cock," she said with a laugh then stuck the girl's arm.

Anna winced. A moment later, rich red blood flowed down the tube and into the bowl. Anna's blood emptied into the vessel. I stared, aghast, at the sight. Anna squinted her eyes and didn't look. Beside me, William was breathing hard. A moment later, the Queen carefully removed the syringe.

"Very good," she said, patting Anna on the head. She nodded to her man who then set about bandaging Anna's arm.

The Queen took the bowl to the drink tray. She lifted a crystal goblet and poured the blood inside. Taking the glass with her, she sat in an ornate chair. She smiled wickedly at Anna who was staring at her.

"Cheers," she said, lifting the goblet in toast. She sipped the blood, closing her eyes as she relished the taste.

Anna bit her lip as she suppressed a scream, and two giant tears rolled down her cheeks.

William moved protectively toward me, his hand brushing my lower back.

"Delicious," the Queen whispered then took a second drink, this time draining the goblet. When she was done, she set the glass aside. Fresh blood stained her lips. "Farm fresh," she said with a laugh then rose. She went to the end of the table and picked up an envelope, which she handed to me.

"Tell Jabberwocky that if he ever comes across any similar products, he always has a buyer." She smiled, her teeth and mouth stained with blood.

I took the package, turned, and headed toward the door. I didn't dare meet Anna's eyes. I didn't dare. I couldn't. I knew what fear and plea for help I would find there. I couldn't permit myself to see it. I couldn't leave her there like that, but I had to. It was wrong to leave her there, but I had to. I was leaving her to unimagined torments, but I had to. Because that was what the job required. Because that was what Jabberwocky asked me to do. I pushed the door open and headed down the hallway.

From the room behind me, I heard the Queen of Hearts's laughter. "What's wrong, Bandersnatch? Don't you want to stay for an aperitif?" she called.

A moment later, William caught up with me.

"Did you know?" I whispered.

"No. I take it you didn't either."

I shook my head.

"She…she drank Anna's blood," William whispered.

"Sanguinarian. That's what it's called. It's a form of black magic." I felt like I was going to be sick. "I will never deal with that woman again. We betrayed that poor girl. We were stupid, reckless thugs. God knows what horrors we just left her to."

Moving quickly, we headed back out into the light. I was never more grateful to see the sky in all my life. Once we were inside the safety of the carriage once more, William pulled me close to him and kissed the top of my head.

My whole body was shaking. "I'll never forgive myself," I whispered.

I looked at William. He'd gone pale. "When Jabberwocky is gone, everything will be different. We'll do business differently."

"Be honorable thieves."

"Yes."

"Is that a promise?"

"Yes. I would never do something like that. Whatever the deal was, it wasn't worth it. That poor girl…"

"Honorable thieves," I whispered, pressing my head against his chest.

"I'm sorry. I'm sorry you had to see that. I'll speak to Jabberwocky. Never, ever again," he whispered, touching my cheek.

I sighed deeply, feeling the terrible weights of guilt and anger struggling inside me. Lifting a box, picking a lock, or swiping a document was one thing. But trading in blood? Jabberwocky had never asked anything like that of me before, and in that moment, I swore it would be the last time.

I didn't know how wrong I was.

BESS CLOSED THE DOOR. SIGHING, she leaned against it, turning to look at me. "He worries me," she said.

I squinted my eyes hard, pushing the memories away. "Just bad luck.

He's fortunate he's not hurt worse."

"You're right," Bess said as she went to clear the dishes.

"Don't worry about those. I'll get them," I told her.

"Nonsense. You've been working all day. Dinah, how about some scraps?" she called. I heard her scraping out our bowls.

I took a deep breath and brushed the tears from my cheeks. I got up. Wordlessly, I took the bowls from Bess's hands and put them in the washbasin. She turned and finished clearing off the table. Taking a cloth, I worked the dirty bowls with the soap, its sharp lemon scent nearly gagging me.

"Lord Dodgson's niece and her family will be coming in from the country to celebrate her birthday. I'm afraid I'll have some very odd hours in the coming days. Please don't worry yourself. If I'm out late and you get scared, promise me you'll ask Henry to stay here with you."

"Alice, you know I can't do that. It's indecent."

With my back turned to her, Bess didn't see me roll my eyes. "I don't know why the two of you don't just go ahead and get married."

When Bess didn't reply, I turned around and looked at her. To my astonishment, a tear was trailing down her check.

"Bessy?"

"You're right," she said sadly. "He always tells me he's trying to save up some money first. Do you think…Alice, do you think he doesn't ask because he knows I'm very ill? Do you think he doesn't ask because he thinks I'm just going to die anyway?"

"Bess!"

"I'm serious."

I set the bowl down and turned and embraced my sister. "No. That's not the case. Henry loves you. He loves you more than anything. He would do anything for you."

"Except marry me."

"He will. He wants to do what's best for you."

She smiled half-heartedly. "It's not like I need a fancy wedding. I just want him…and maybe a little holiday."

"A trip to Bath to take in the waters? They have good doctors there. I'm sure someone could give us a suggestion for you, Bessy. Between me and Henry, I'm sure we could raise the money."

"Perhaps if I paint some Chinese vases."

"There you go. Let's make a plan. We'll start saving now. By next winter, we'll have you and Henry married, and we'll all go to Bath to take in the waters."

This time, Bess smiled for real. "I love that idea."

"Then we'll inform Henry of the plan tomorrow."

"Inform Henry? That he has to marry me?" Bess asked with a laugh.

I smiled. "Indeed, and at your wedding, you will wear the best hat London has ever seen."

Bess laughed. "Alice, you're mad indeed."

"I certainly hope so. All the best people are."

9

PIERCED RED THINGS

I LEFT EARLY THE NEXT morning while Bess still slept, taking with me the blueprints and the dress box the Countess had given me. Stepping out onto the streets of London, I spotted a lamplighter passing through snubbing out the last of the flames as the sun began to break over the horizon. The cobblestone streets were clouded with fog. The haze made everything thick and blue.

I slipped down one side street after another, my hand clenched around the White Queen, as I finally made my way to Caterpillar's house. At least, it was his house now. As I stared up at the third-floor window, my mind rushed back in time. How long had it been since I'd first set eyes on the place?

BESS AND I WERE NINE and ten when we found ourselves standing before Jabberwocky's massive home for the first time.

"Is this the place? This big house?" Bess whispered in my ear, her hand gripping mine tightly.

"This is the address," I said, looking down at a scrap of paper in my hand.

Mustering up my nerve, I went to the door and knocked. I remembered the sound of it, how it seemed like my knock had echoed through an empty space. A few moments later, a man in a dark suit answered the door.

"Yes?"

"Mister Northman told us to come to this address," I said, handing the paper to him.

"Mister Northman?"

"Yes. A man asked Mister Northman to send us here."

The doorman nodded. "Very well. Come in," he said. I held Bess's chilly and damp hand. We stepped inside the cavernous place. The foyer of the house was dark save a few candles that had been lit in the circular chandelier that hung overhead. The place seemed like it had been washed in gray. Everything felt muted, lifeless. "Wait here," the man said. Taking a candelabra with him, he headed upstairs.

"Alice, we should run away from this place. This is a bad place," Bess had whispered.

"Run where? Back to the workhouse?"

Bess shifted nervously. I stiffened my nerve as we waited. We stood still, like we were frozen in place, as we waited. We stood there so long that my feet grew sore. At last, Mister Mock, whom we would later come to know as Jabberwocky, appeared on the steps.

"Well, if it isn't the little sisters. Alice and...what was it again?"

"Bess, Your Grace," my sister said with a curtsey.

The man laughed. "Alice and Bess. Very good. Most people call me Jabberwocky," he said.

"That's a very odd name," I said before I could stop the words from tumbling out of my mouth. I slapped my hands on my lips but it was too late.

He laughed then bent down to look at us. "Yes, it is," he replied generously. Even then his hair was already turning silver, but it still held a blonde hue. His face was not unkind, but it had a hawkish look. His skin was mottled with liver spots and deep lines ran across his forehead. "Now, do you know why you're here?" he asked. "What did Mister Northman tell you?"

"Nothing," I replied, lowering my hands, "except that our contract was bought out by the tall man who'd come through the factory the week before."

"The tall man," he said with a laugh. "Do you remember seeing me?"

We both shook our heads.

"I saw you," he said, pointing to me, "unsticking that gear before the machine crushed your friend's hand."

I thought back. The week before, Davin had nearly lost his fingers when a machine malfunctioned. I'd seen the loose part amongst the working gears and had knocked it into place before the wheel could take his fingers.

I smiled abashedly.

"No bragging? I like that. I asked Mister Northman about you. He told me that you have a gentle sister. Turns out that I had a job for a pair of girls just like you, and Mister Northman owed me a favor, so here we are. Miss Alice," he said, eyeing me skeptically. "I want to give you a test."

"Yes, sir."

He grinned. "Come with me," he said, motioning for us to follow him. He led us through the hallways to the back of the house. Each hallway, each door, seemed to lead to another. Every room seemed to be painted in the same odd blue-gray color. The place felt like a tomb.

A moment later, however, he pushed open a door to reveal a small garden at the back of the house.

"Oh, how lovely," Bess exclaimed.

"Isn't it? And my apple tree is just as full as can be. Do you like apples, girls?"

We both nodded.

"Very well. Let's see if Alice can win you one," he said. From inside his belt, he pulled out a dagger. He handed the blade to me. "Not five minutes

79

after you saved your friend, I saw you peg a rat with a rock from three meters away. You have very quick hands, Alice, and Mister Northman tells me you also have a quick mind. Now, how can you do with apples? Do you think you can hit that one all the way at the top of the tree?

"Yes, sir. Apples are much easier. They wriggle less than rats."

Mister Mock laughed. "Let's see then."

I took a step forward and aimed. I knew that no matter what, my mark had to be perfect. My future, I felt, depended on it.

I lobbed the dagger.

There was a crunch, and a bright red apple fell from the tree, skewered by the dagger.

"Well done," Mister Mock said, clapping his hands together.

He retrieved the apple and his dagger. He cut the apple in half and gave half to me and half to Bess.

"Very good," he said, wiping the blade clean. "You'll need a bit of training up, and you and your sister will have to stay here—can't have you living with the boys—but I think those big blue eyes and quick little fingers will serve me well. Do you understand me, Alice? Do you know what job I have for you?"

I looked at him. Bess, who was chewing her apple happily, suddenly stopped and stared at Mister Mock.

"I do, but my sister cannot do such work."

He smiled at Bess then reached out and gently patted her head. "Look there," he said, pointing to an upstairs window.

To my surprise, there was an elderly woman sitting at the window. She was rail thin and looked to be a hundred years old, but she smiled kindly and waved to us. "My mother is very old and needs a companion, Miss Bess. She's quite ill. She hardly knows her own name and doesn't recognize anyone from one day to the next. I need someone with a giving heart to look after her. Mister Northman said you can read?"

She nodded. "Oh, yes. And I'm very patient."

Mister Mock nodded. "No doubt you are. My dear mother used to love to paint. Perhaps you can tempt her to it again. So, girls, what do you say? Do you suppose we could make a deal?"

"Shall we try it?" Bess whispered to me.

I looked back at Mister Mock. I was only ten, but I knew what life he was offering me. I'd work the streets, picking pockets and lifting goods. It wasn't honest work—it wasn't even safe work—but it would mean a comfortable life for Bess. My sister had nearly died the winter before in the cold bunkhouse. She was too gentle to wrangle machines and chase rats out of her food bowl. If we had stayed with Mister Northman, my sister might have died. Our parents were dead. I hardly even remembered them anymore. We had no one else. I didn't want to be a pickpocket, but for Bess, I could do anything. We'd have a room in a fine house, my sister reading books to an old woman, sitting beside the fireplace all winter long. There wasn't anything in the world I wouldn't do to win that kind of life for my sister.

"Bess will work in the house. Always. You promise?" I asked Mister Mock.

He smiled. "Yes."

"Then we agree."

"Very good. Come along then. Let's get you settled."

I looked up at Madame Mock. She smiled nicely once more. Bess waved happily to her. I hoped beyond all reason that things would work out and that the price would not be too great.

I STARED UP AT THE window of the third-floor bedroom. Knocking on the front door felt entirely too obvious. I turned and headed down the nearby alley until I reached the back garden wall. Securing the blueprints on the strap across my back, I tossed the dress box over, then gripping the stones, I pulled myself up.

I dropped into the garden of Jabberwocky's—formerly my own—house. Everything was as it had been. Setting the box against the trunk of the old apple tree, I grabbed a branch and climbed up. The limbs stretched to the ledge. Moving carefully, I slipped off the branch and onto a ledge along the building. I eyed the decorative flagstones jutting from the side of the house. Getting a tight grip, I scaled the wall to the third-floor ledge. I shimmied to the window. I peered inside to find William still asleep. Balancing carefully, I pulled my knife then slipped it along the window frame, maneuvering open the lock. Moving carefully, I pushed the window open and slid inside.

William sighed and rolled over but didn't wake.

A small fire burned in the fireplace of Mister Mock's old bedroom. The room was warm and comfortable. William had changed the furnishings and linens, leaving the sense of the familiar and the new all at once. The room was sparse save his desk. Moving quietly, I sat down at the desk and began looking through the papers. He was corresponding with an airship pirate, moving opium from the Orient into London. He'd had some dealings with an apothecary in Cheapside leaving an itemized bill behind. The desk was littered with the expected items and a lot of literature on the Crystal Palace. The only piece of information that did catch my eye was a dispatch from a merchant in Virginia talking about inventory that was scheduled to be delivered via the airship *Siren* on April twentieth, two weeks earlier. Something about the way it was written, the vagueness of description, felt suspect. I looked through the rest of the papers but there was nothing of importance.

Rising slowly, I moved silently to the bedside and looked down at William.

How sweet he looked as he slept. His lashes were so long, but they'd always been like that. I remembered those lashes on the little boy version of him, the little boy who'd fallen instantly in love with me.

I stared at his lips, remembering the feel of them against mine.

Pain rocked my heart.

Had he really left me for nothing more than this life? This house? This wealth? Was I so easily cast aside?

But guilt nagged at me. In reality, who had done the casting? Wasn't I just as much to blame?

I sat down on the side of the bed, not bothering to be gentle, then stroked the lock of hair that fell just over his ear back into place.

"Your security is terrible. I could have murdered you five times by now," I said gently.

He startled awake, gasping as opened his eyes.

"Alice?" he whispered. Without thinking, he reached out and took my hand. The sweetness of it, the look of warmth in his eyes, caught me off guard. "Alice."

It wasn't the reaction I'd expected. I'd expected he'd brandish the dagger under his pillow to prove me wrong, or make some smart comment, or get up and move away angrily. Instead, the look on his face was much different.

"I…I let myself in. Through the window," I said.

He didn't even crack a smile. "I dreamt, you know, of waking up to your face in this house, in this room. I dreamt of waking up to your touch. Alice," he said. He lifted his hand and touched my cheek, his fingers trailing gently down to touch my lips.

"Yes, well, we're at an impasse on that, aren't we," I said, rising. I had to get away from him or I was most certainly going to kiss him.

"Please, let's talk about it," William said, sitting up.

"What's there to talk about?"

"It's not too late for you to change your mind. You wouldn't have to come back into the life. You and Bess can move back here. This is your home. I hate that you're living in that hovel above the dress shop. I hate that Bess is too poor to marry that hatter. It's not too late, Alice. We can just do it over again."

I went to the fireplace. Was he right? Could I come back? Could we do it over again? How many times had I regretted my decision? How many times had I felt the pang in my heart that I, not William, was at fault?

William rose and joined me, wrapping his arm around my waist, pulling me close. "Alice. Please. You know I never stopped loving you. And you never stopped loving me. Come home to me."

"Why are you doing this job for the Queen of Hearts?"

"What?"

"The job. The job that has a very high probability of getting one or both of us shot or put in the stocks. Why? Why did you take the deal? What went wrong between you and her?"

"I...it's complicated."

"I'm reasonably intelligent. Try me."

"Alice," he said, but he said no more. I realized that no answer was coming.

I pulled away. "You see. This is why. This is why I won't come back.

Nothing but darkness surrounds this life." I turned and looked at him. "Get dressed," I said then turned and headed toward the door.

"Where are you…are you leav—"

"Of course not. Dark deals or no, I'm not going to leave you to hang for whatever it is you've done. I'm going downstairs to see if Maggie will cook me some breakfast," I said then slammed the door behind me.

Too close.

Too close that time.

Too close to saying yes.

10
INSIDE A RAINDROP

"IF YOU SAY IT AGAIN, I'll stab you," I said as I struggled to adjust the formal gown. The bulging bustle of fabric on my backside made my lower back itch, and my corset was too tight. A proper lady's gown indeed, but I wondered how anyone who dressed in *proper* fashion got anything done. I touched the brim of my tiny top hat. It, along with my parasol, were the only pieces of the outfit I actually liked. Of course, the parasol had a feature that allowed me to slip the White Queen into the shaft to serve as a handle. Leave it to the Countess to think of that.

"All I said was that you look lovely. I hardly think that's a stabbing offense."

"Shows what you know," I replied as I eyed him sidelong. He had changed into a fine suit and wore a black top hat. I both hated and loved being there with him. My conflicting emotions made me cranky.

"Tickets," said a man standing just outside the door of the Crystal Palace.

"Good morning," William said politely and handed the man our tickets.

The man stamped the date on the tickets then handed them back. Nodding, he motioned for us to enter.

Taking me gently by the arm, as a gentleman ought to do, William escorted me inside.

While the Crystal Palace's ornate structure, made of glass and iron, towering several stories high was a sight to behold from the outside, nothing quite prepared me for the marvels inside.

As we entered, a cacophony of sounds reached our ears. The sweet melodies coming from a stand of self-playing harps, the screech of monkeys, the hum of machines, and the sounds of hundreds of voices rolled to our ears all at once.

The structure had been built around the tall ash trees that had stood in the park. They still stood standing tall in the middle of the structure. Fountains lined the center promenade. The crowd gasped and stepped back as a group from Africa passed on their way toward their display, lions on leashes walking in front of them. Not far behind them, a man wearing a straw hat jogged past pulling a rickshaw, two laughing—and elegantly dressed—ladies inside.

I gasped as a man flew overhead on wings made of lightweight material. To my great surprise, he flapped his wings, the metal of the clockwork bones and joints revealed when the sun overhead struck him just right.

William chuckled. "Shall we take it all in?"

Barely able to breathe, I nodded.

"Now, there is *my* Alice," he said softly. "Her curious eyes open wide."

I smiled. "It's a wonderland."

In that moment, I could hardly feel angry at him. He had tricked me to bring me back into his circle and was being completely obtuse on why he was in this predicament in the first place, but I loved being there with him.

"Ladies and gentleman, ladies and gentleman, come see these wonderful clockwork delights," a gentleman called from the German exhibit. He was standing in front of a curtain.

William and I stopped to look.

"How many of you have ever loved a dear pet and lost one? A dog, madame? Perhaps a scrappy little alley cat, sir? What if you could own a pet that never died? What if you could own a pet that would always be there for you, save time when it came for a patch or two? Behold," the man called, and pulled the curtain away, revealing an odd little zoo. Inside a display of cases were all manner of creatures, and all of them made of metal.

The crowd gasped.

"The clockwork menagerie," the man said. "Fine German craftsman-ship. Each creature made to order by our tinkers," he said then pulled a clockwork cat—a fine looking machine made of striped metal to make the animal appear as if he were a tabby cat—from the display. He set the cat on a show platform.

"The cat has been designed with optics to navigate your home and behave just like a living creature. Simply press this lever to activate your feline," the man said, pressing the lever. The cat's eyes opened wide. They were the color of aquamarine gems. It stood and twitched its mechanical tail, then sat again once again and began licking a metal paw with an equally metal tongue.

"Does it meow?" a child called, her mother and father looking on.

"Only if you like," the man said. "Just wind the small crank here, and your kitten will cry for his…oil!"

Everyone laughed.

The man worked the crank and a moment later, the clockwork cat let out a loud meow. He picked the creature up, holding it just like a cat, and walked in front of the crowd so everyone could see and touch it.

"It even purrs. Madame, would you be so kind as to give him a scratch behind the ears?" he said to me.

I looked from the cat to William then back to the cat again.

Reaching out, I stroked my hand across the metal ear of the cat. A purring sound erupted from the little creature and then, a moment later, the clockwork feline smiled, revealing a row of wide, square teeth.

I laughed. "He's smiling like he just had a bowl of Cheshire cream."

The crowd gathered around me chuckled.

We took in the presentation then turned back to the main thoroughfare.

"Look," William said, pointing to the massive stone sphinxes that stood at the entrance of the Egyptian exhibit. We headed inside to discover all manner of fine artifacts on display: papyrus scrolls, an ornate sarcophagus, and lapis lazuli jewels.

In my childhood dreams, I'd imagined myself a treasure hunter. I envisioned myself exploring the pyramids in Egypt, a crumbling map in hand. I envisioned myself outsmarting ancient curses on chests of pirate treasure or unlocking the secrets of the lost Atlantis. But such adventures could only be had in my imagination. In reality, Bess and I had been left to the workhouse after our parents had died of a wasting disease. Jabberwocky had saved us from certain poverty, but at what cost?

As I walked beside William, taking in the delights, I thought about my path. William was right. It had been my choice to leave. I didn't want the life. I didn't want to do the job anymore. But he too had chosen. He'd picked the life over me. Yet I could go back. It wasn't too late.

I shook my head. I didn't dare think about it anymore. After all, this was a job, not a date. I scanned the area around us. There were four guards at the main entrance, two at each of the six side entrances, and one of Victoria's men in each display in addition to whatever security the international groups had brought with them. I looked the guards over in the Egyptian exhibit. They eyed the visitors, looking for pickpockets. The admission price, however, kept the common street ruffians away. Yet their eyes were keen. No one would get past them alive.

We left the Egyptian exhibit and carried on with our tour. The Great Exhibition took up two floors with a third, half floor, above. Several windows were cranked open overhead to let the heat out. The tops of the trees inside the building nearly reached the windows.

"There is a line to see the diamond, but it disperses at lunch time. We'll go then," William whispered in my ear.

"So, does that mean you won't be buying me lunch? I am, after all, putting my life on the line for you. Doesn't that earn me at least a ploughman's platter?"

William laughed. "Afterward. I promise."

Next, we took in the Chinese display, marveling at the lanterns, paintings, and myriad of painted vases. As we passed, I picked up all the pamphlets they had available showing the artwork.

"For Bess?" William asked.

"Yes. Several of her customers have remarked on the vases. She wanted to try her hand at them."

"Replicas will catch her a fortune. She should come see them herself."

"I'm sure she can render the images from these well enough," I said, looking down at the papers. In truth, the cost of entrance into the exhibit was well beyond what we could afford. On top of that, Bess could not walk to the exhibition. She'd need a carriage, and unless we found someone with one to spare on her behalf, there was no way for her to get there without risking her health.

William frowned, guessing at what I had left unspoken. In his expression, I saw his frustration. "You're so stubborn, Alice," he scolded me then under his breath. "Wouldn't life with me, back at home at the manor, with some means at your disposal, be a better life for you both?"

"Here I am, finely dressed and seeing wonders I could never afford on my own, but I'm about to commit a crime against the crown. The trade-off hardly seems worth it."

"Alice—"

"If something happens to me, you will be responsible for taking care of Bess. You remember that."

"I promise I will protect you, nothing will—"

From somewhere in the building, a massive clock chimed, drowning out his words. I sighed with relief. Whatever it was he was planning to say, I didn't want to hear it.

I glanced up at a nearby clock. It was the lunch hour.

"Shall we?" I said, looking in the direction of the British display.

William nodded and said nothing more.

We joined the main thoroughfare once more. Each country had beautiful displays tucked into alcoves along each side with other interesting displays along the center of the walkway. There was a colorful display of glassworks in the Austrian exhibit, Turkish textiles and rugs, and models of ships and silks from India. We bypassed the American display where an airship had been docked at the center of the exhibit. A presentation was underway showcasing the use of helium. As well, the display of Colt revolvers was getting a lot of attention. Eventually, we reached the queue for the Koh-i-Noor. The diamond, just as the Countess's schematics had revealed, was sitting in what looked more or less like a bird cage on a pedestal. I eyed the crowd. There were less than twenty people in line in front of us. Two guards kept watch on the diamond. The gem was sitting on a red pillow.

"It's very large, but it doesn't have any sparkle," a lady in a fine dress complained to her husband as they walked away from the exhibit.

"That's because it's cursed," her husband replied.

My brow furrowed. "The diamond is cursed?" I asked William.

He nodded. "The diamond is bloody. It was a *gift* to Victoria from her *admirers* in India."

"So, you mean, we stole it," I said under my breath.

He nodded.

I frowned. How typical. But somehow the notion made me feel a little better. If the diamond had been stolen in the first place, if it didn't really belong to Her Majesty, then maybe that made all this better. Maybe.

As we moved forward, I eyed the layout of the space. The diamond had its own alcove off of the main thoroughfare. It was open on two sides. There was nothing else on display in order to accommodate the large crowd.

One of the guards yawned sleepily and pulled out his pocket watch.

The wooden podium—which I remembered from the schematic was

really a safe—was strong enough to hold the weight of the heavy metal cage. As we drew close, I saw a steel box under the pillow on which the diamond sat. Under that was a levered panel to drop the box, diamond, and pillow inside, into the pedestal.

"Madame? Sir?" the exhibitioner called, motioning for us to come forward.

William and I came to stand in front of the diamond. It was large enough to take up the entire palm of my hand, but it was oddly cut. The

shape was a strange sort of oval. As the passing lady had said, it didn't shimmer at all.

"A bit lackluster," William said.

The exhibitor barely batted an eyelash. It was apparent he'd heard the comment a hundred times already.

I leaned forward to look more closely. Then, pretending to swoon a little, I exclaimed loudly then tripped against the display. I reached out and grabbed the bars as if to steady myself. I threw some of my weight against the display. It didn't move. The diamond never budged.

"Madame," the exhibitor exclaimed, reaching out for me.

William, pretending to be distracted, waited a moment before he noticed my distress. "My dear," he called, reaching out for me.

To my surprise, both guards—who had but a moment ago looked

half-asleep—and the exhibitor arrived at once.

"Oh," I exclaimed with a gasp. "Oh, gentlemen! Oh my! I'm so very sorry. I suddenly saw black spots before my eyes and swooned."

The exhibitor breathed a sigh of relief. Nothing had moved. The diamond had not shuddered a bit.

"I'm so very sorry," I said, batting my big blue eyes at them.

The guards regarded me closely, looked at one another, and with a nod, returned to their posts.

"Oh, I'm so very sorry," I said, looking from the exhibitor to the guards. "How terribly embarrassing."

"Are you all right, pet? What happened, love?" William asked, fanning my face.

The exhibitor smiled generously. "It's a long line. And it's quite hot in here, isn't it? No damage was done. Perhaps your wife needs a bit to eat," the man said to William.

As he spoke, I scanned around. Several gentlemen, all in similar black suits, had suddenly come very near the display. They exchanged glances with the guards then disappeared, presumably back into the crowd.

William smiled at the man. "Excellent idea, my friend."

"There are many food tents outside. But everyone is raving about Alexis Soyer's Symposium of All Nations at the Gore House just across the street. Hot meals. Food from all nations," the exhibitor suggested. "I've heard it's very good. Or you can get a ginger beer, a pickle, and a stale bun down that way," the man added with a wink.

William laughed. "Thank you, sir," he told the man then took my arm. "Come along, my dear."

At that, we headed away from the display.

"Well?" William whispered once we were a safe distance away.

"The pedestal seemed to be welded to the ground. The bars are solid steel. Nothing shook. Nothing moved. It's sturdy. It's a safe, just as the schematic showed."

"Guards are lax," William commented.

"The ones we saw. There are guards mingling amongst the crowd. But they are all wearing the same black suits. There," I said, motioning casually toward a display French jewels. "The man carrying the sketchbook. And there," I said, tilting my chin toward another display of lamps.

"I see," William said. "What now?"

"We need to see what's done with the diamond at the close of day."

"Then let's have some lunch and return for a second look."

"Pickles, bread, and ginger beer?" I asked with a grin.

"I don't know. I'm not sure what *Alice in the red dress* would prefer, but my Alice was always ready to drink a ginger beer."

Unable to stop myself, I grinned at him. "And what about you?"

"I want *Alice in the red dress* to have everything she deserves. Come, let's try Soyer's Symposium. We'll eat Chinese food. I've heard they eat with sticks."

"Chopsticks."

"Chopsticks. Shall we try?"

"And ruin my fine red dress?"

We both laughed then headed outside, away from the vendor tents, and toward the Gore House.

The sun was shimmering brightly. It was a fine day. I held onto William, soaking in his warmth, remembering the curve of his arm.

"I missed you," William said softly. "And you must admit, you missed me too."

"Yes. I've missed you too."

"Alice, won't you consider—"

"What does the Queen of Hearts have over you? Why are you doing this?"

"There was a job. I…I botched it. I owe her."

"Too easy an answer. Botched it how?"

"It's compli—"

"Yes, it's complicated, you've mentioned that. William, I've known you since you were ten years old. Nothing about you is this complicated, at least, not so complicated that you cannot tell me. Who knows you better than I do?"

William sighed. "No one. But Alice, I…I just can't."

"Until you tell me the truth, then we are at an impasse."

"Alice, I'm trying. You don't even know how hard I am trying here. I am doing everything—"

Just then, however, I felt a shadow fall in too close behind us. I pulled the White Queen out of the parasol handle and turned.

William broke off midsentence.

Behind me, I found Jack and Rabbit.

"Alice," Jack said with a smile, lifting both hands in the air and stopping cold.

Rabbit, his mop of white hair glimmering in the sunshine, smiled up at me, a mischievous look on his face. It was then I noticed that he was eating a pickle inside a bun. Now, how had he managed that if they were for sale inside the exhibition? He was still wearing the oversized, expensive-looking, waistcoat.

"What is it?" William asked.

"You're needed," Jack told him.

"Now?"

"Yes."

"But I was just going to take Alice to—"

"The crew of the *Siren* is here. There is some…trouble."

William paused. I could see the crush of conflicted feelings wash over him as his expression changed. He needed to go. It was obvious. But I could see that he also realized the timing could not have been worse. "Alice, I—"

I wanted to understand. I really wanted to be sympathetic, but the moment had felt so good. I wanted to go on living it. In truth, I had missed him desperately. And I was very certain that I was about to get to the truth. But once more, Jabberwocky's ghost was back to haunt us. I couldn't stand it. "Just go," I said coldly.

William dug into his pocket and pushed a coin purse at me. "Please get some lunch. Spend it all. Buy anything you want. I need to attend to this matter, but I'll be back. Meet me at six o'clock? The exhibition closes at seven. I'll meet you inside?"

I slipped my blade back into the parasol handle, popped the parasol open, and turned back toward the Great Exhibition building.

"Alice," William called to me.

"Fine," I replied.

As I walked off, I heard Jack's voice.

"Sorry. It's just the captain stabbed two people already. Rabbit, run off and tell them we're coming."

I frowned and kept going. Well, William was right. He had shown me what life would be like if I went back to him.

Disappointing.

11
FOOL ME ONCE

BACK INSIDE THE EXHIBIT, I sat sipping a ginger beer and watching the diamond most of the afternoon. My analysis of the security was right. On first blush, the guards had seemed sparse and rather lax. That was, of course, a false assumption. There were many—*many*—security officers in black suits canvassing the place. I nibbled at my stale bread, the crumbly mess spoiling my fancy red dress, and tried to focus on the diamond. Instead, my mind drifted off to consider how everything had gone so terribly wrong. And whenever I posed that question to myself, a single night came to mind.

The job was supposed to be a simple one.

"Here is the address," Jabberwocky had said, handing a slip of paper to me. He nodded to William. "Just the two of you. The banker left for Cambridge this morning. According to the maid, the safe is on the second floor behind a painting of Queen Victoria. Go now."

"And what are we looking for?" William asked.

"Documents."

"Surely he'll have many papers on hand. How will we know which documents?" I asked.

"Just take all the papers you find in the safe. Leave anything of wealth. Just bring any papers," Jabberwocky answered.

I frowned. It was unlike him to be so vague. But after that bloody business with Anna and the Queen of Hearts, I had begun to suspect Jabberwocky's grasp was beginning to slip. Deals were going bad all around town. A new crew was starting to encroach on Jabberwocky's territory, and he seemed reluctant to do anything to stop it. William had been patching the holes in the business and keeping things afloat. Jabberwocky seemed...distracted. I eyed him closely. Madame Mock, Jabberwocky's mother, has degraded terribly in her final years. At the end, she knew no one, called Bess by her late sister's name, and repeatedly asked for her mother. Jabberwocky seemed increasingly disorganized and distracted. I worried for him.

William nodded then turned to go. He only paused when he saw I wasn't coming.

"If the papers are not in the safe, we'll need to search the office. Sir, you know you can trust us. What are we looking for?"

Jabberwocky frowned then said, "The papers will contain the name Anastasia Otranto."

"Who is Anastasia Otranto?" I asked.

"That's all you need to know. See to it."

"Yes, sir," William said from behind me.

"Yes, sir," I echoed.

Jabberwocky mumbled under his breath but never looked up at me.

I frowned and joined William.

"Nothing we can't handle," William said confidently as headed out into the streets of London.

The sun was setting and there was a chill in the air. It was late fall. Winter was coming. Already the cough in Bess's chest had started to rattle. I frowned and tried not to think of it. I pulled my coat tighter around me.

"You want to take a carriage?" William asked.

I shook my head. "Let's walk. I want to think. I don't like this. We don't know anything. This is sloppy."

"Ransom's crew tried to take over another block today. Jabberwocky…I told him but he didn't answer. Instead, he asked me to have some marmalade sent to his office. That was all. Jack and I are meeting with Ransom tomorrow. This job…something seems odd. Anastasia—whatever the name was—who is she?"

"I don't know."

William sighed heavily. He kept clenching and unclenching his jaw. What were we going to do? If Jabberwocky was slipping, it meant huge problems for all of us.

William and I worked our way across town until we came to the banker's small townhouse. It was already dark, and the lamplighter had not yet arrived at this end of the street. The houses all along the row seemed empty, including the residence in question. We walked confidently to the front door. Doing so would put any passersby at ease. If we acted like we were supposed to be there, they would assume we were. I pulled out slim lock pick tools from the top of my boot and worked the lock. A moment later, the door opened, and we headed inside.

We paused a moment, closing the door quietly behind us. We stood still in the darkness, listening for any sounds of trouble.

The little house was quiet save the ticking of a clock. Nothing and no one was stirring.

William pulled out a pistol and a dagger, and we headed upstairs. William checked each room to ensure it was empty. We made our way to the second-floor office. The small space had a large desk littered with papers. The walls were lined with bookcases filled with leather tomes and other oddities.

I pulled the heavy drapes closed then lit a candle that was sitting on a desk.

There was a substantial amount of coin stacked there, but I didn't touch it. I scanned around the room until I spotted a painting of Queen Victoria.

I motioned to William, and we headed toward the painting. It was attached to the wall but opened on a lever.

"Sorry, Your Majesty. Don't look," I told the image in the painting then pulled the lever.

The painting flapped open to reveal a safe built into the wall. I pulled a desk chair closer to the wall and climbed up so I could put my ear on the lock. I leaned in and began to slowly turn the tumbler. My ears pricked up, and I listened intently as the mechanism rolled as I turned the dial. It took some doing, but a few moments later, we both heard the telltale click as the safe unlocked.

"Got it," I whispered.

William lifted the candle so I could have a better look inside.

Therein were numerous jewelry cases, gold watches, and stacks of coins. I moved them aside and pulled out a leather envelope. William held the candle while I untied the fasteners. I pulled out the papers from inside. I quickly noted a deed and a birth certificate with the name Anastasia Otranto thereon as well as some papers from the Bank of Scotland.

"Thieves," a voice said from the office door.

William and I looked up to see a small man standing there. He was holding a lamp in one hand and a pistol in the other. From his dress, it was apparent he was the banker who was supposed to be in Cambridge.

I shoved the papers back into the envelope.

"Go," I whispered to William.

I jumped from the chair as William turned and flung open the window.

"Stop or I'll shoot," the man said.

I cast a glance back. He was aiming his pistol at William.

"No need to get excited. You won't find anything valuable missing," I said.

William turned slowly.

"What? What are you talking about? What do you have there?" the banker asked. His glanced at the envelope. His eyes went wide. "Put those down," he told me harshly, but his body belied the confidence he tried to exude. His hand was shaking, his finger squeezing the trigger too tightly. Just a tremor more, and we'd have a serious problem. He kept the gun on William, who was advancing slowly on him.

"Just stay calm," William told him, putting on a false Irish accent. "No one needs to get hurt. Put that gun down."

"Stop. Stop right where you are or I'll shoot you both," the banker told William.

Moving slowly, William pointed to the pistol in his own hand. "I seriously doubt you're a faster shot than me. Why don't you set that gun down?"

The banker looked at me. He was pale and trembling. "Put those papers down and go or I'll shoot him."

"Let's just take it easy," William said, stepping closer toward the banker.

"I said stop," the man exclaimed.

William advanced quickly.

The man took a step back and fired.

William gasped as the shot grazed his shoulder.

A second later, the banker aimed again.

I had no time to think.

Dropping the pouch, I pulled the White Queen from my belt and threw her.

My aim was true. The dagger slammed into the man's face, puncturing his eye.

His hold on the gun went soft, and the pistol fell to the floor. The man stood upright for a moment, a look of shock frozen on his face. Blood dripped from his eye. Then, he slumped to the ground.

William and I stood perfectly still.

The gunshot would be enough to raise an alarm. We needed to get out of there.

Collecting myself, I grabbed the file folder and rushed across the room. The banker lay dead on the floor. Blood pooled around his head. I reached down to pull out the dagger. She came loose with a spray of blood that covered my hands and forearms. "I…I killed him," I whispered.

"Alice. Alice, I'm shot," William said.

"He's dead. I've killed a man."

"You did it to save me. You saved my life, Alice."

"But…he's dead." My stomach quaked so hard I almost vomited. I turned to look at William. He was holding his shoulder. Blood oozed from between his fingers. "William," I whispered aghast, shocked to see him bleeding.

"We've got to go. Now. You have the papers?"

"Yes."

"Then let's go," William said.

Pulling myself together, I nodded. We rushed back to the window. Not taking a moment to even consider it, we both leaped to the street below. I felt a sharp pain in my ankle as I landed, but the call for the constables was already audible in the wind.

"This way," William said.

Gritting my teeth, I ran behind him. We ducked down alleyway after alleyway. We raced quickly through the darkness. My heart pounded hard in my chest and over and over again I heard the voice inside my head screeching, *you've killed a man, you've killed an innocent man.* After we were half the city away, we stopped a moment in a darkened alcove. Wordlessly, William pulled off his coat. His shirt was drenched in blood. He was bleeding profusely, and his face had gone ashen. In the moonlight, I looked over the wound. I pulled a scarf from around my neck and wrapped it around his shoulder.

"Come on," he said, then we headed back into the darkness until we reached the small flat where William lived.

My heart thundered in my chest. I was a pickpocket. Nothing more. I wasn't a killer. But still, my hands were covered in blood. I had killed a man. And for what? For a handful of papers?

When we entered the flat, William motioned for me to follow him to the kitchen. There he pulled off his shirt and grabbed a pitcher of water. He motioned for me to put my hands over the basin. "You'll need to inspect my wound, to make sure the bullet just grazed me, but you need to clean your hands first."

He pulled some astringent off the shelf and splashed it all over my hands and forearms then poured water thereon. Grabbing the soap, I scrubbed my arms and hands until I felt like my own skin was going to come off.

"Alice, I think that's enough," William said, gently setting his hands on mine.

"I killed a man," I whispered, turning to look at him. I hadn't realized it then, but tears were streaming down my face.

William wiped my tears away with his thumb. "You did it to save me."

"I just...I couldn't let him kill you. I love you," I whispered.

"Our job always comes with risk," William said as he sat down. Wincing, he began to unwind the scarf from around his shoulder. "Risk of getting caught. Risk of getting jailed. Risk of a deal going bad and finding yourself on the wrong end of a fist. Risk of getting stabbed or shot. Risk of getting killed." He dropped the bloody scarf on the floor. "We choose between a free life, this life, or servitude in a factory or at some bloody job shoveling shit."

"And in this moment," I said as I gently poured water onto his wounded shoulder, "this is preferable?"

"Can't stand the smell of horse shit," William said with a grin as he mopped sweat off his brow.

In spite of myself, I laughed. I cleaned the blood away from his would as best I could then washed the wound again. After that, touching as gently as I could, I inspected the injury. "No bullet. It just grazed your shoulder."

"There," William said, pointing to a tin of salve on a shelf nearby.

Understanding his meaning, I grabbed the tin, applying the sticky substance to the wound, then grabbed one of William's clean shirts sitting nearby.

I raised an eyebrow, tilting my head in apology, then ripped the shirt. Carefully, I bandaged his shoulder. As I worked, the scene replayed over and over again in my head. What had happened? How had everything gone so wrong? I didn't know anything about the man save he was, in fact, a banker. He was a banker who had papers Jabberwocky needed. Just who was Anastasia Otranto anyway?

"Alice?" William said finally.

"I just," I said then sat down in the chair near him. "William, I…"

"I know," he whispered. I realized then that he was sweating profusely and his skin had turned milk white. "Alice," he whispered weakly.

"You've lost too much blood. I need to put you to bed," I said.

Lifting him gently, putting his good arm around my shoulder, I helped him to bed.

For as much time as William and I spent together, I had never stepped more than two feet into his living quarters before. They were sparse but neatly kept. He had a stack of books sitting at the end of his bed. And tied to the banister on his bed was a dried rose. I remembered then that it was a rose I'd given to him just that past summer. I smiled when I saw it.

"I need to send a messenger," I said. "I need to let Jabberwocky know we got the documents, but there were complications. And I need to send a note to Bess, to let her know she shouldn't expect me until tomorrow."

"Tomorrow?"

"I can't leave you alone. I'll need to watch you in case you need a surgeon."

William looked carefully at me but didn't comment. "Second-floor flat, west end. There is a boy there."

I grabbed some paper off William's table and quickly composed two notes then headed out. In the flat on the second floor, I found a room full of children and one exasperated looking mother. She made a half-hearted attempt to smooth her hair and straightened her apron when she saw me.

"William needs a messenger," I told the woman. "He told me—"

"Charles," the woman called toward the rowdy gaggle.

One of the older boys came forward. He nodded to me. "William needs these messages delivered. Two addresses," I said, handing the boy the papers.

"Yes, ma'am," he said. The boy took the notes, pulled on his coat, and headed out. I watched him go. When I looked back, I noticed the mother was standing with her hand outstretched.

I set a pile of coins in her palm then went back upstairs.

When I arrived, William was mostly asleep. I set my hand on his forehead. No fever. In fact, he felt chilled. I pulled another blanket over him.

"Alice," he whispered.

"Don't worry, I won't leave you alone."

"It hurts. I have powder by the sink. In a green bottle. A spoonful in a glass of water."

I rose and went to make the concoction. I found the bottle with the sharp-smelling herbal powder. I mixed it with some water then took it back to him.

"Where did you get this?" I asked.

"A witch," he said with a laugh as he struggled to sit up.

"Of course," I replied, smirking.

"I'm serious," he said with a grin. Taking a drink, he handed the cup back to me. I helped him settle back into bed. I sat down beside him, brushing the hair away from his eyes.

"I'm sorry, Alice," he whispered. "You're too good for this life, too smart. Definitely too good for me."

"You're sorry? You're the one who got shot. Jabberwocky is the one who should be sorry. And I'm no one special. I'm not better than you. I'm nothing more than a guttersnipe, just like you."

"A smart one, and a beautiful one," he replied, taking my hand into his. "And you're my someone special."

"William," I whispered, warmed by his words. But even so, the image of the dead man flashed through my mind once more. My stomach shook.

William looked closely at me. "I know. I know you. Things will be different now. Your soul cannot abide it," he whispered.

Moving carefully, I lay down beside him, setting my head on his chest. I pulled the White Queen out of my belt and let her drop to the floor. She rolled out of reach.

"I love you, Alice," William whispered into my ear.

I closed my eyes and listened to the beating of his heart. "I love you too."

A few hours later, there was a knock on the door.

I rose quietly and went to the door. The boy I'd sent with the messages was standing there.

"Sorry I took so long, miss. Ran into some...problems," he said, pointing to his red and puffy eye.

"On no! Are you all right?"

"Oh, sure. The other boy ran home crying to his mother," the kid said with a laugh, but then he turned serious. "Something odd going on, miss. There was no one at The Mushroom. Not even the guards. And at the house, well, there was a pretty lady there with curly blonde hair. The woman you sent the other message to. She said you and Master William need to come right away. She looked like she'd been crying."

My heart froze.

Bess.

"William?" I called back.

"I heard. I'm getting up."

"Thank you. And sorry about the eye."

The boy grinned, nodded, then ran off.

"Help me dress?" William called after I shut the door.

"Let me check the bandage first." I gently looked over the wound. "It's not bleeding anymore, but we'll need to change this wrapping soon."

"After," he said.

I nodded then pulled a fresh shirt from his wardrobe.

My emotions tumbled over themselves. Something was wrong. Bess was crying. A man was dead. And I'd spent the past hours lying in William's bed. I didn't think it was possible for a person to feel fear, rage, despair, anxiety, and deep love all in one moment. It was a dreadful sensation.

I grabbed the parcel with the stolen papers, slipped it inside my jacket, then helped William button his coat.

"We won't say anything," William said, motioning to his shoulder, "until we see what's going on."

I nodded. If something had gone wrong with the job, if Jabberwocky had been arrested, William's wound would give him away.

We headed back outside. It was very early morning. The sun was just about to tip over the horizon. The sky had an odd haze of light yellow and gray. Anxiety racked my stomach. Something was terribly wrong. The feeling, married to my despair over what I had done, made my heart hurt.

"I'll never forgive myself," William said as we walked. I could tell by the look on his face that he was about to attempt to lighten the mood. I took the bait.

"Why not?"

"Because I lay beside you half the night and didn't even try for a kiss."

"You don't have to try," I said, leaning in to give him a peck on the cheek.

William grinned. "Well, it wasn't exactly a kiss that came to mind," he said. His eyes met mine. William and I had been friends since we were children. Somewhere along the way, we'd fallen in love. But the transition had been smooth. As of yet, we'd never quite crossed the line into a more physical relationship. It wasn't that I didn't want him. It was just that the timing had never felt quite right.

"Well, the next time you get shot, make sure you take a chance," I said, leaning in to kiss him on the lips. I lingered there for several moments, kissing him gently, tasting his sweet lips. The lingering taste of the tart herbal concoction spiced his kiss.

After the moment passed, William took my hand. "Next time. For certain," he whispered, kissing the top of my head. He took my hand and we made our way back. When we exited the alley that led to the big house, we were surprised to see a number of carriages parked outside. Two of Jabberwocky's guards stood outside the door.

We approached cautiously.

I cast a glance at the windows. Guards milled around everywhere, but in the third-floor window, I spotted Bess.

She must have raced downstairs because, by the time we reached the front door, she was there. She flung the door wide open.

"Oh, thank goodness," she exclaimed.

The guards nodded to William and me as we passed.

Once the door was closed, I set my hands on Bess's arms and looked into her eyes. "What's happened?"

Tears streamed down her cheeks. "Jabberwocky is dead."

"Dead?" William whispered. "How? Who?"

"No one. Well, doesn't look suspicious. Late last night I noticed his lamp was still lit. You know I usually check on him. I thought maybe he'd fallen asleep with it on. I found him on the floor. Oh, Alice, he's dead," she wailed then wrapped her arms around my neck, burying her face in my neck. She wept softly. "We're finally free," she whispered so only I could hear.

"Alice," a voice called from behind me then.

I turned to see Jack exit the parlor, closing the wooden doors behind him. For just a moment, I spotted several other people collected inside. All were heavy hitters in Jabberwocky's establishment.

"We were waiting for you and William," Jack said.

I looked deep into William's eyes. I shook my head.

William stared at me.

"Alice..." Jack said, reading between the lines. "The others were waiting for you, in particular."

As Jabberwocky had wanted, they would turn to me next.

No.

I couldn't.

I wouldn't.

"Give us a minute," I told Jack. He nodded and went back inside.

"Alice?" Bess whispered.

I turned to William. "I can't, especially not after tonight."

"That was Jabberwocky's mistake. It won't be like that going forward. You'll make new and better choices."

"Yes," I said, then took Bess's hand. "I'm choosing to not go through that door."

"Alice," William whispered. "Don't do anything rash."

"I'm not. And you shouldn't either. Bess and I have money saved. I know you do too. We could strike out on our own, the three of us. We're all free now. All three of us. We owe no one anything. Jabberwocky saved all three of us, taught us, protected us, and turned us into his creatures. But we don't have to live this life anymore," I said, turning toward my sister who was looking at me with hope in her eyes.

"Alice, are you mad?" William whispered. "You stand to inherit everything. His house. His wealth—"

"His problems."

"We'll turn the business around. Make something different out of it."

"And how will that go with those gathered in there, those with an investment in what Jabberwocky created? There will be even greater bloodshed. Now is the time. Now we must decide. If we walk through that door, more lives will be in our hands, more souls like Anna. Have you forgotten?"

"I haven't. You're right. It will take some time to change things, but we can change things. It doesn't have to be forever. Just for a time until we fashion our affairs the way we want them."

I turned at looked at Bess. While Jabberwocky had been good to us, we'd both lived in a sort of lull, a strange indentured servitude. And now, we could be free.

"Have they taken his body away yet?" I asked Bess.

She shook her head. "No, but they'll be here soon."

I turned back to William. I pulled the packet of papers from inside my coat and handed it to him. "I won't go in there."

"Alice, you aren't leaving me any choice," William replied.

I shook my head. "I'm giving you every choice. Come upstairs with us and say goodbye, then we begin anew."

"And do what?"

I shrugged. "Craft watches? Start a school? Go into shipping? Anything but that," I said, pointing toward the door.

I could see the struggle on William's face. "Right, you're right," he finally said with a nod. "Jabberwocky was like a father to me, but you're right. I just…I can't let his affairs end in disarray. I'll set things to right, and then we'll do just as you suggest. We'll create a new world. A new life," he said, smiling brightly.

And in that moment, his eyes were so full of love and life that I believed every word he said.

Until it turned out to be a lie.

I LOOKED INTO MY EMPTY mug of ginger ale.

"Miss?" a man said then, shaking my shoulder. "Miss? Terribly sorry, but the exhibition is closing for the day." I looked up to see one of the security guards standing there.

I cast a glance up at the clock. It was already seven o'clock. He hadn't come. Just another lie.

"Oh my! I guess I lost track of time," I said with a smile. "Is it too late to see the Koh-i-Noor?" I asked, rising.

The guard looked toward the exhibit. "Afraid they're tucking her in for the night."

I followed his glance, then watched as a guard worked a heavy lever that lowered the closed steel box, in which I presumed the diamond resided, into the display case.

"Alas, I waited all day for the line to go down. I can't stand so long on account of my health," I lied. "Don't tell, but I'm afraid I dozed off," I said with a whisper, trying to look as delicate as I could possibly muster, but mostly I was trying to bide my time.

Once the steel case was lowered into safe, a heavy metal lid slid over it. I could hear the sound of locks rolling into place. Once the diamond was secure, the guard dropped a heavy velvet drape over the display cage.

"Lunch time. Everyone scatters for something to eat. Try then," the man advised.

I nodded. "Thank you. Again, my apologies. Terribly embarrassing," I said then turned and headed toward the exit.

There was no sign of William anywhere.

It was then that I made up my mind. I'd have nothing more to do with stealing Victoria's gem until I had some answers. And since William wasn't talking, I'd have to find them myself.

12
BEWARE OF
AIRSHIP PIRATES

I SLID INTO A SEAT in the corner of Rose's Hopper, a popular spot for airship jockeys, and waited. It had only cost me a few of the coins William had given me for an expensive lunch to buy the nod I needed from the barmaid when the crew of the *Siren* entered. They looked like just another motley crew of pirates. But their attire—cavalry boots and cowboy hats—bespoke their origin even before they opened their mouths. The captain was American. Some of his crew had accents common to the southern states. They were a rough crew, all of them wearing fresh bruises. They drank quickly and talked loud. Typical Yanks. I rolled my eyes, dropped a coin on the table, and exited. I went to one of the benches below the airship platforms and sat amongst the crowd of travelers gathered there.

And then, I waited.

It was just after dark when the *Siren's* crew exited the pub and headed toward the tower lift. The captain was still inside drinking. I kept one eye on the tavern and another on the ships overhead. Not half an hour later, the burner on the *Siren*, a mermaid ensign on her balloon, came to life. The airship's balloon filled with orange light.

I rose and headed slowly toward the lift, spinning my parasol as I walked.

A few minutes later, the airship captain exited the tavern and headed toward the platform. I matched my step so I'd be able to ride up with him.

As he neared the lift, the tower guards eyed him warily and said nothing. They usually conducted passengers upward. This one, however, they let pass by.

"Miss. Next lift. We'll take you up," one of the guards called when they saw me.

I ignored him and walked forward.

"Miss," the guard called again. It was clear that he was watching out for the welfare of a poor lady about to trap herself in the lift with an airship pirate.

I gave the man a quick, knowing glance then inclined my head.

Understanding, he turned away. I entered the lift behind the inebriated pirate.

"Hey, where did you come from?" he asked, scowling at me.

"Sussex," I replied, pulling the lift door closed behind us.

Confused, he looked at me like I was mad.

"Well, are you going to take us up or not?" I asked.

"English girls," he said with a laugh then worked the levers.

The large gears overhead turned. We headed upward.

"English girls. What about us?"

The man turned and looked at me. He had dark hair that stuck to his forehead. He reeked of alcohol and sweat. His white shirt was stained at the armpits. His cowboy hat sat low on his forehead. He grinned at me. "Nice parasol."

"Do you like it? It has a special feature. Shall I show you?"

He rolled his eyes.

Moving quickly, I pulled the White Queen from the parasol's handle and set it on his throat.

"Nice, isn't it? I'm not sure *all* English girls have a parasol like this one, but you might want to be careful in the future, just in case. Now, be a good lad, and stop the lift."

He looked at me side-eyed. His expression was low and mean.

"I know you're considering tossing me off the lift. Reasonable idea but a bit extreme. You've nothing to fear from this English girl. I just have a couple of questions then I'll be on my way."

"And why should I tell you anything?" he growled, but he slowed the lift to a stop anyway.

"Well, there is the dagger. And mainly because it won't cost you anything to answer."

"Who sent you?" he asked through gritted teeth.

"No one. I sent myself."

"Why?"

"I already told you. Just have a quick question then we'll part ways."

"I saw you in the tavern. If you wanted to talk, why didn't you just buy me a drink?" he asked with a smirk.

"Too crowded, and I'm not much of a drinker."

"Well, now you've piqued my interest. Lower the dagger. I won't toss you over today," he replied. I could tell from the look in his eyes that he was telling the truth.

I lowered the White Queen. "I want to know what cargo you carried on the twentieth of April."

He raised an eyebrow at me then smirked. Rummy pirate, that smirk was more charming than it should have been. "It was for an associate."

"I know it was for Caterpillar. I just want to know what kind of cargo it was."

"You're asking the wrong question," he replied with a grin.

"I am?"

"The last person who put a blade to my neck wanted to know where that cargo went, not what it was."

It was my turn to raise an eyebrow at him. "And where did that cargo go?"

"I didn't answer him. Why should I answer you?"

"Because I'm sure I'm much prettier. And because I'll say please."

"You are much prettier, so I'll play along. But I'll only answer one question. Push the subject further, and I'm afraid we'll have to come to a disagreement, no matter how pretty you are."

I considered my options. "All right. Where did the cargo go?"

"Well, I didn't haul it. But word gets around. From what I hear, it went back where it came from."

"Which was?"

"That's two questions."

"Well, your answer was less than specific."

He laughed. "Fine. San Francisco."

"Who transported it there?"

"Now that, clearly, is the second question."

"Yes. You're right."

"Someone who doesn't work cheap but works fast and quiet."

I frowned. "Why did Caterpillar return it?"

"That's three questions," the airship captain replied then leaned back, folded his arms, and looked closely at me. "You're right, you sure are prettier than that grumpy gent with the silk turban."

I grinned then slid the White Queen back into the handle of the parasol. I pushed open the door to the lift. We were between platforms three and four.

I turned to the pirate. "Thank you," I said, curtseying politely.

The pirate tipped his hat to me. "Ma'am."

Without waiting further, I jumped from the lift to the third-floor platform and headed back downstairs. I didn't look back to see if the pirate had his pistol on me or not. Something told me I'd given him something better than another victim to shoot…another tall tale to share at the pub. I opened the parasol and worked my way back downstairs.

So, the Queen of Hearts had wanted something, something William had procured then returned? Very odd. No wonder she was furious. That kind of woman always gets what she wants. And that kind of woman was the most dangerous.

Now I just had to figure out what the cargo had been.

I HEADED AWAY FROM THE airship towers toward home. It was already dark. As I made my way home along the cobblestone London streets, I twirled my parasol in my hand. The sun had set, so there was no need for the parasol, but it was still fun to twist it around and around as I played everything over in my mind.

Already I could see a way to take the diamond. I would need to visit the exhibition at night and get some supplies, but it could be done. I could do it, but should I? Why was William bargaining with the Queen of

Hearts? Bargaining and then changing his mind.

I turned down a side street where I knew boys looking for work were known to linger. The group of grubby little guttersnipes stood huddled under a streetlamp. They eyed me curiously as I made my way toward them.

"You lost, lady?" one them asked as I approached.

I grinned. "No. I need someone to run a message."

They looked at one another and then back at me and my fine red gown.

"Do you?" the eldest of them asked, eyeing me over.

"Yes," I said with a sigh. The shakedown was, of course, inevitable. "Don't get ideas. Appearances are often deceiving. Now, before I have to stab one of you to make my point, who can run to Twickenham?"

The boys laughed.

"Me," one of them said. "I know the barge master. I'll get a lift."

I pulled a small notepad from the reticule dangling from my wrist and wrote a quick note, sealing it inside a small envelope.

"Lady Frances Waldegrave, Strawberry Hill House."

"The Countess?" the boy asked, his eyes wide. Apparently, her reputation preceded her.

I nodded then handed the boy some coins and the note. He stuck them in his pocket, nodded to me, then turned and headed in the direction of the river.

"Good night, lads," I said.

"The Countess?" I heard one of the boys whisper to the others.

"You idiots. Don't you know who that was?" another asked.

"Who? The lady in red?"

"Yes, you dolt. That was Alice."

"Alice?"

"Alice…the Bandersnatch."

The other boys were struck silent.

Grinning, I turned the corner and headed home.

13

A MAD TEA PARTY

"ALICE! YOU'RE LATE AGAIN," BESS said the minute I opened the door. "And what are you wearing?"

"Lord Dodgson gave it to me. He didn't want me to go to the Great Exhibition looking like a servant. It's just a loan."

"Oh! Did you go? You must tell me everything. First, go knock on Henry's door. Tell him it's time for supper."

I headed across the hallway and rapped lightly on the door.

Henry opened the door a crack.

"It's time to eat," I said flatly.

"What are you wearing?"

I frowned at him then turned to go back.

"Alice, please come inside a minute."

I sighed then turned back. Today was turning out to be exhausting.

Henry opened the door and led me inside. His flat was a jumble of ribbons, fabric, buttons, bows, and all manner of sewing paraphernalia. But that was nothing new. When he wasn't busy getting himself in trouble, Henry was a prolific hatter, and his works were stunning. He closed the door behind me.

"Pretty," I said, picking up a hat that was decorated with peacock feathers.

"I don't know what to say. You haven't told Bess anything?" The lines around his eyes wrinkled with worry.

"No, because it appears you learned your lesson this time."

"Not about me, about you and Caterpillar."

"I'm just working a job."

"That I got you into. Alice, I'm so sor—"

"Don't be. He used you to drag me back into his world."

"Alice, you need to be careful."

I waved my hand dismissively. "I'm always careful."

"I'm talking about with Caterpillar."

I looked Henry in the eyes. He was like a brother to me. He was the first friend we made after we'd left Jabberwocky's house. It had been love at first sight between him and Bess. But he didn't know William. That was one problem. The other problem was that while he didn't know William, he did know that I carried a broken heart and that William was the cause.

I sat down. On the table in front of me was an enormous top hat upon which Henry had situated a teapot. I lifted it. It took some effort, but I was able to balance it on my head.

"Who in their right mind orders a hat like this?" I said.

Henry laughed. "You answered your own riddle. Who in their right mind? It's for a tea party for a ladies' group. They've ordered six of them."

I laughed out loud.

"Alice...are you still in love with that man?"

"No. I mean, I don't know."

Henry shook his head. "The things I've heard about him..."

"That's the life, not the man. The man is one thing. Caterpillar is quite another."

"There is not one without the other."

"There is. But he has to choose. And he did. He chose that life."

"Then what are you doing back in the middle of it? For me? If it's just for me, then—"

"No. For him."

"Why?"

"Because..." *Because I don't want anything to happen to him. Because I still have hope we can be together. Because...I still love him.*

Henry sighed, picked up another of the teapot hats and put it on, then sat down beside me. He patted my hand. "I know, Alice. I know."

"You know, you're entirely right. This is all your fault," I said with a joking smile. "Your mistake is forcing me to face my past, forcing me to finally examine my buried feelings. It's all rather heart-wrenching. It's almost enough to make me hate you."

Henry smiled softly. "Very sorry."

"Don't gamble again," I warned him. "Next you'll have me dealing with my parents' death. Don't you know it's easier to repress such feelings? Ignore them. Bury them. It's the best way, don't you know?"

"I do. Why do you think I gamble?"

I laughed, but then turned serious. I took Henry's hand in mine. "Be done with it. Please. We'll find another way."

He nodded. "I am."

"You said that last time."

"I know. But the only person I was hurting last time was me. Now, I see, there is more to my life than just me."

"So you promise?"

"Yes."

"Has Bess seen these hats yet?"

"I don't think so."

I leaned over then and picked up a third hat. This one featured a stack of teacups at the top. "Let's go," I said, taking the extra hat with me.

Laughing, Henry and I headed across the hallway. The moment we walked inside, Bess burst into laughter.

It was the best sound I'd heard all day.

14
CLOCKWORK HEARTS

I WOKE UP THE NEXT morning to a knock on the door. I opened my eyes sleepily. Bess was already at the door.

"Yes?" I heard her whisper.

There was a muffled reply.

Sleepily, I sat up.

A boy stepped into the room and set a large crate down on the door. He tipped his hat to Bess, put an envelope in her hands, then left.

"What is it?" I asked drowsily.

"I don't know," Bess replied, pushing her curls away from her face. "It's for you."

I rose and took the envelope from her hand. Inside were two tickets for the Great Exhibition and a note:

Tickets for Bess and Henry. She should see the wonders for herself. Carriage will arrive at 9.

I'm sorry I missed you yesterday. Meet me at eleven at the big house?

W.

I paused, unsure if I should lie or not, then handed the tickets to Bess.

"What are these?" she asked.

"Tickets for the Great Exhibition. For you and Henry."

Bess gasped.

"A carriage will be here at nine to take you."

Without thinking, Bess turned and opened the door, rushing across the hall to Henry's flat.

Dinah wove through my feet then paused to investigate the box, sniffing it daintily.

I bent down to take a look.

There was a tab on the lid that read, *pull me.*

Motioning for Dinah to move back, I pulled the tab. The lid clapped open then all four sides of the box fell away.

Lying inside was the clockwork cat from the German exhibit.

Dinah meowed at it.

Reaching out, I turned the lever, activating the mechanical creature.

Its wide aquamarine-colored eyes popped open and it rose. It looked around the room then turned and faced me. Once more, it gave me that wide toothy grin.

I laughed.

"Oh! Oh, my. What is that?" Bess exclaimed, her eyes full of wonder.

She sat down on the floor to look at it more closely, Henry following into the flat behind her.

"Our new cat, of course," I replied, reaching out to stroke the back of its ear.

When it started purring, Bess laughed out loud. The cat turned and smiled at her. "Just look at that smile," Bess exclaimed.

Dinah meowed questioningly at it.

"Where did you get it?" Bess asked.

I cast Henry a passing glance, but the expression on his face told me he'd already riddled it out.

"An old friend."

"Which old friend?"

"That is a conversation for another time."

"Alice," Bess said, with a soft warning in her voice.

"Later, Bess. I promise."

Bess and stood beside me. She pushed a stray hair behind my ear then smiled, patting me gently on the cheek. "Okay, Alice. When you're ready. Now, what are we going to name this new creature of yours?"

The cat turned to look at me. "Cheshire...we'll call him Chess for short."

"Chess," Bess said. "Well, what do you think, Dinah?"

Our little calico, her yellow eyes wide, meowed once more then stepped toward the clockwork cat and rubbed her head under its chin.

To our surprise, both cats started purring.

We laughed.

"What time is it?" I asked.

"Nearly eight," Henry replied, pulling out his pocket watch.

"The carriage to take you to the Great Exhibition will be here by nine. Can you go?" I asked Henry.

"I wouldn't miss it for the world. I just need to deliver the tea party hats first."

"Oh dear, Alice," Bess exclaimed. "I'm so excited. You must thank your friend. But whatever am I going to wear?"

"Take the red dress."

"The one Lord Dodgson lent you?"

I nodded.

"But what if I spill something on it? I can't risk ruining it."

"It will be fine."

"But what if," Bess said then paused. "What if I get one of my nose bleeds?"

I wrapped my arm around my sister. "Take a handkerchief and don't worry. Today is going to be a beautiful day, and you are going to see the wonders of the world."

At that, Chess meowed.

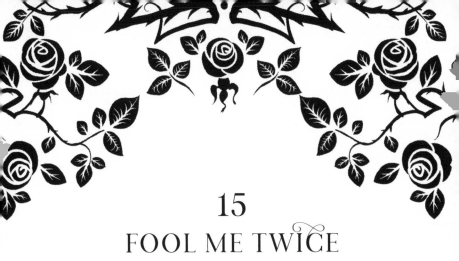

15

FOOL ME TWICE

IT FELT STRANGE TO KNOCK on the door of the house I'd considered my home most of my life. But there I was, just before eleven, standing in front of Jabberwocky's big house wondering why I was outside and William was inside. But then, of course, I knew the answer. It was my fault, my choice. I'd put myself there.

I knocked.

A few moments later, Mister Sloan, Jabberwocky's butler, opened the door. "Alice," he said with a smile. "Come, my dear. William told us to expect you. He's in the library."

"Thank you."

"It's good to see you. Maggie said you were by the other morning. Sorry I missed you. How is Miss Bess?" He tried to hide his worry when he asked about my sister, but it was plain on his face all the same.

"She's doing very well," I said.

"Ever-pleasant girl, your sister," he said with a nod. "Now, let me tell Maggie you're here. She's been cooking ever since William said you were coming." The look on his face revealed something unexpected: hope.

I smiled, nodded, and then went to the library. There, I found William looking over some papers. I wasn't able to get a good look, but I'd sworn I'd seen the word *Aphrodite*.

"And what do we have there?" I asked.

He shook his head, folded up the paper, and set it aside. "Nothing," he said then turned and opened a chest sitting on his desk. From inside he pulled out a glass bottle and set it on the table.

"What's that?"

"Powder. We mix this with a spritz of water and it creates a powerful acid that can melt just about anything. Of course, if we breathe it in we'll be dead in a matter of minutes. If we touch it, it will melt our hands off. So, suffice to say, handle with care," he said then set the powder back in the box and closed the lid. "Did Bess receive the tickets?" he asked, turning his back to me as he fussed around with the contents on his desk. Was he shielding himself from my reaction?

"Yes. Thank you. She was very excited. It was thoughtful of you to include a ticket for Henry as well. I'm sure he'll be a much better companion to her with all his fingers intact."

"His debt is forgiven. I saw to it. He doesn't have anything to fear."

"Why did you do that?"

He turned and looked at me. "Why wouldn't I? Did Bess know who sent the tickets?"

"She suspected."

"And what did she say?"

I remember Bess's pitying glance. If anyone knew my true heart well, it was my sister. And worse, it was William. I smiled then shrugged.

He grinned. "Did my gift arrive intact?"

"It did. Do I dare ask how you procured it?"

"I'm offended. I purchased it, of course. I thought you'd approve more that way."

"I do. But why does that matter?"

"It matters that you approved. It matters that you liked it. Do you?"

I swallowed hard. "I do. Thank you. I named him Chess."

William smiled. A moment later, there was a knock on the door. Maggie stuck her head inside. "Would you like your lunch in the dining room, sir?" she asked, pausing just a moment to smile brightly at me.

"Can you bring it here? You won't be able to eavesdrop as well, but Alice and I have work to do."

She frowned at him. "I never…Well, I'll just bring the serving cart, then. Hello, Alice."

I grinned at her. "Hello, Maggie."

"Now," William said, dropping onto a couch near the front window. "What do you think? Night job?"

I sat down beside William. The sun shimmered in through the window. The light and dark flecks of blue in his eyes sparkled. He seemed so easy, so delighted to have me there. It felt so comfortable between us. In that moment, I did something I probably shouldn't have, but I did it all the same.

I took William's hand in mine. "What's happening here?" I whispered.

"What do you—"

"Not between you and the Queen of Hearts or the business or anything else. Why am I here? What is this all about?"

William leaned forward and took my other hand in his. "This past year has been hell for me. I can't live without you. Life is just…it's nothing. There is no point to any of this. I know you can't come back. I'm trying to make good on the promise I made the day Jabberwocky died. I'm trying to tie up all the loose ends, and then I want to be done with it."

"What?"

"I'm going to pass the business to Jack. I'm trying to get out. I have been all this time. It was just such a disaster. Jabberwocky was in over his head, much more than we knew. There were so many problems to clean up. You wouldn't come back. I couldn't just leave. The man was like a father to me. But I'm close now. This job…"

My heart pounded in my chest. "Why didn't you just tell me?"

"I thought I could finish it. I nearly had the matter settled. Jabberwocky was indebted to the Queen, and I needed to clear that debt. Until that was done, there was no way I could leave. I had a plan, but it fell apart. The diamond is the last key to my freedom."

I shook my head. "The Queen of Hearts is a maniac. You've seen with your own eyes what she really is. Don't tell me you can just forg—"

"Never," William whispered. "But I have no choice. To get back to you, I must pass through her. And I would do anything to get back to you."

"William," I whispered. I closed my eyes. Understanding, then pain, racked me. So much of this was my fault. I had left William to deal with this on his own and had judged him for it. It was just after all we'd seen, I couldn't imagine staying a moment longer in the life than I had, dealing with creatures like the Queen of Hearts.

William and I had seen what the Queen of Hearts did to Anna. What we'd seen in that room was nothing. I'd last seen her just days before the job with the banker. I'd never forget the night Jabberwocky had woken me well past midnight with a job that had rocked me to my soul.

"ALICE," JABBERWOCKY WHISPERED SO NOT to wake Bess. He rocked my shoulder softly. "Alice, wake up."

"Sir?"

"William is downstairs. I need the two of you to go, now, and take a package to the Queen of Hearts."

"What? Now?"

I looked at Jabberwocky. He looked ashen. He'd been sleeping less and less these days. Something was terribly wrong here. "Get dressed," he whispered then left.

Moving quickly, I pulled on a pair of black pants and a shirt. This time, I equipped every weapon I owned, keeping the White Queen on hand. I quietly slipped out of the room only to hear William and Jabberwocky on the third-floor landing above me.

"Alice," Jabberwocky called.

He looked down the stairwell and motioned for me to come upstairs.

When I reached them, I looked briefly at William only to discover that he was as confused as me.

Jabberwocky motioned for us to follow him up the narrow stairwell that led to the roof of the house.

Once we reached the roof, both William and I were surprised to see an airship hovering above the house. Airships were prohibited from coming low into residential neighborhoods. The airship had its lantern off. I eyed the balloon. In the dark of night, it glowed a dim orange color. The insignia looked like Medusa. I didn't know the ship or its captain, but the whole thing just felt wrong. A rope ladder wagged in the breeze.

"The ship's captain will take you to the Queen's manor. She's expecting you. Deliver the package and come back immediately."

"Excuse me for saying so, but the last time we—" I began, but Jabberwocky cut me off.

"Do your job, girl, or you and your sister will be on the street. Get that package delivered and take what she gives you. I don't care what you see," he replied sharply.

In all my years of living and working for Jabberwocky, he'd only ever been kind to me and Bess. I was shocked.

"Yes, sir," William said then headed up the ladder.

I stood staring at the man who'd practically raised me.

"Mister Mock," I said softly. "You're in trouble. What can I—"

"Deliver the package," he said, his tone softening. "Just…just deliver the package."

He said then turned and headed back inside.

I climbed up the ladder behind William and slipped aboard the airship.

Without a word, one of the crew pulled up the ladder and the captain, who looked like he'd prefer if I didn't notice him, turned the airship toward the Queen's manor.

"Bloody hell," William whispered.

"I was asleep. How in the world did you get here?"

William shook his head. "Messenger woke me up, told me to come at once. I arrived the same time the airship got here."

"Do you know what the package is?"

William shook his head.

We stood at the side of the ship and watched as the streets of London slipped past us as the airship made its way to the Queen's abbey. William took my hand. His fingers were cold. He stood clenching and unclenching his jaw. I eyed the crew. None of them were making eye contact.

We arrived just a short while later, the gothic gables of the Queen's abbey taking shape on the horizon in the moonlight. The captain maneuvered the ship above a grassy spot on the grounds. Moving deftly and quietly, the ship lowered as far to the ground as she could without damaging the rudder.

"Get out here," one of the crew members told us as he tossed a rope ladder over the side of the ship. "We'll lower the box."

Without another word, William and I climbed down the ladder. We stood in the grassy space to the side of the Queen's abbey. From inside, I saw the flash of lamplight. I felt the strange sensation that we were being watched. A moment later, I heard an odd clicking sound. I heard the clank of metal coming from the garden. A moment later, three sets of red lights appeared in the darkness.

"William," I whispered then pulled my blade.

I looked overhead. The crew had opened the galley and were lowering a box to the ground. One of the crew members stood on top the crate, guiding it gently to the ground.

William had pulled his pistol and stepped between me and the strange lights. There was so much wrong here I didn't know where to look. I heard the manor door open. Overhead, the crew of the airship held pistols on the red lights, the manor, and us.

A moment later, under the glow of the moonlight, I saw the glint of metal. Three very large automatons emerged from the garden. The red lights had been their optics. They were moving toward us. One couldn't help but notice the maces, swords, and axes they carried.

"Halt," a voice called.

I turned to see the Queen's henchman—the man in the black turban we'd met on our last visit to the Queen with Anna—moving toward us.

The automatons stopped at once.

Once the box was lowered to the ground, the crewman unharnessed the box, lashed the harness around himself, then waved to his crew. I heard a winch click on, and the rope quickly retracted.

"Carry this inside," the henchman instructed the metal men.

The automatons, while their movements were very awkward, moved forward and lifted the box. They marched slowly toward the front door.

I nodded to William, and we followed along behind.

"Jabberwocky has sent his favorite pets," the man in the turban said as he walked beside us toward the house. "Do you know what's in the box?' he asked with a smirk.

"We don't care. Your Queen has something for us. We'll have it and be gone," William said grimly.

"Your transport left you behind," he said, waving a hand overhead.

Overhead, the airship lifted quickly as her balloon filled with hot air. It glowed like a lantern against the night's sky. The ship turned and headed back toward the city. Fabulous.

"Nice night for a stroll," William replied with a false smile.

The henchman smirked then motioned for us to follow him inside. The massive creatures carried the box with ease to the second floor. There we followed them down a long hallway. Some of the doors on this floor were open. Men and women, most of them drowsy, many of them naked, lay on beds or the floor. Some were drinking or smoking opium. Others seemed to be lost in a stupid slumber.

I had decided it was better if I kept my curious eyes to myself when I noticed a familiar face. Sitting glassy-eyed at the end of a bed, staring into an empty fireplace, was Anna. At least, I thought it was Anna.

Unable to stop myself, I went to the door. "Anna?" I called.

The girl didn't look up. It was her, but it wasn't her. She was so very thin. Her cheekbones and shoulders protruded like they wanted to burst from the paper-thin skin that held them in.

"Anna?

"This way," the Queen's henchman said.

"Alice," William whispered.

I stared at the girl. There were cuts all over her forearms and on her neck. "Anna?"

William grabbed my arm. "Come on," he whispered then pulled me away.

Anna turned and looked at me. Her big blue eyes had gone dim. A half-dead thing looked back at me. She stared at me for a moment then looked back at the empty fireplace.

"This way, pets," the man with the turban called sharply.

"What happened to that girl?" I demanded.

"The Bandersnatch should not ask questions," the man replied then turned to the automatons. "Stop," he called to them.

The machines stopped with a jarring halt that rattled the box.

For a moment, I swore I heard a groan come from inside.

I cast a glance at William.

"Stay here," the man said then entered a room with a set of double doors.

From inside, I heard the Queen of Hearts's shrill voice. A moment later, the man opened the door.

I was surprised to see the Countess exit.

She eyed the box, then William and me. She gave us both a knowing look then headed down the hallway. I turned to watch her go.

The henchman motioned for the machines to enter. "Put it there," the man said, pointing to spot on the rug in front of the fireplace. "Then return to your posts."

Their heavy footsteps clomping, the machines stomped awkwardly into the room.

William and I watched as the automatons set the box down with a thump. This time, I clearly heard a groan.

"Keep it down or I'll have your head," the Queen called.

The machines turned and left the room, William and I moving out of the way of their red-eyed stare. I wasn't certain how the optics worked. I knew they had limited visibility and limited cognition, but they were able to make their way without any problem. Their heartless manner frightened me. So much brute strength with no soul seemed a terrible thing to me.

"As usual, Jabberwocky's timing is miserable. I suppose Bandersnatch and Caterpillar are here?"

"Yes, madame," the henchman answered.

"I wasn't asking you," she replied sharply, her voice filled with annoyance. "Don't stand in the doorway, Jabberwocky's favorites. Come in. I'm almost done."

Done? Done with what?

Reluctant to move, and more than curious as to why the Countess had been there, I entered the Queen of Hearts's boudoir. The room had a large medieval style canopy bed with velvet drapes. There was a round table, many chairs and chaises, and elaborate wardrobes. The walls were lined with tapestries that depicted images I didn't at once recognize. The heroes and settings looked foreign. Mongolian, perhaps? Persian? I wasn't sure. I eyed the room, looking for a clue as to why the Countess had been there. I found it in the form of an old book sitting on the table. There was nothing written on the spine, and the book had the ragged appearance of a journal. What was the Countess doing mixing with the Queen? What hold did she have on everyone?

As we moved further into the room, my eyes also sought out the Queen. Around the corner from the elaborate bed was a fireplace. Sitting in front of it was a copper wash basin. Long white legs dangled over the sides of the basin. William stopped as soon as he spotted her.

The Queen laughed.

"Caterpillar, you spend your entire day with tarts' breasts dangling in your face. Afraid to see a proper lady bathing? Or are you afraid that your Bandersnatch will see the lust on your face when you take in my beauty? I don't know how you do it, Alice. I'd be so jealous I'd have to murder every tart who pushed her tiny tits in my lover's face, whether she took his eye or not, just out of the principle of it."

I looked at William. Neither of us knew how to respond.

"No reply? Very well, then. Bandersnatch, be a dear and fetch my robe from the chair."

Shaking my head, frustrated with the entire situation, I rounded the end of the bed. I tried to avert my eyes, simply grabbing the robe and getting only close enough to hand it off, but I couldn't help but catch a glimpse of the Queen. But more than that, I caught a glimpse of her bath.

I stopped and stared.

"What is it, Bandersnatch?" the Queen asked with a laugh. "Want to join me?"

The copper washbasin wasn't copper at all. It was glass. The reddish orange sheen had come from the liquid inside. She was bathing in blood.

The Queen laughed.

"You've gone positively pale. Hearts, you see," she said, then I heard a splash.

Against my better judgment, I looked. The Queen grinned at me as she sat in her bath of blood holding a human heart in her hand.

"Why do you think they call me the Queen of Hearts?" she asked with a laugh.

I stared at the heart.

"Look at my face," she whispered.

I couldn't take my eyes away. Bobbing on the surface of the bath water were at least a dozen human hearts.

"Look at me," she demanded, her voice shrill.

I looked from the bath to her. I inhaled sharply. She looked like a girl no older than sixteen. She was even more beautiful, more radiant, than she'd been the first time I'd seen her.

The Queen laughed. "Now, give me my robe."

I held it out to her.

The Queen of Hearts rose. Blood dripped down her body. Her skin was as pale as milk, but her body was beautifully formed, almost like she'd been carved out of marble.

"Aren't I beautiful?" she whispered.

I didn't know what to say.

"Well!" she demanded.

"Yes," I replied.

"The most beautiful woman you've ever seen?"

I thought over her question. A flash of my mother's yellow hair, the color of sunflowers, falling in ringlets and the sound of her laughter tumbled through my mind. An image of Bess followed it. No. She wasn't the most beautiful woman I'd ever seen, but I thought it best not to say so. "Yes."

"Humph," she replied, recognizing that I had lied. She slipped on her robe. As she belted the robe, she headed toward the table where the old journal was sitting. I couldn't help but notice that she left bloody footprints in her wake.

"Now, let me see," she said as she eyed over the table. "Ah yes," she said, picking up a small case which she then took to William who, I noticed, was doing everything he could to not look at her. "Here you are, Caterpillar. Now, let's see what you think. Am I the most beautiful woman you've ever seen?" she asked him. She winked at me then unbelted her robe and let it drop to the floor.

William looked at me, his face twisting with anguish. Steeling my heart, I nodded to him.

He looked at her. "You are very beautiful. You look...different."

"Yes. I do look a bit fresher, don't I? Quite a neat trick the Countess worked out for me. She's very good about things like that. But you didn't answer my question, Caterpillar. Am I the most beautiful woman you've ever seen?"

William smiled at her. "You are beautiful. But no."

"No?" she asked. She ran her hands sensually over her breasts. "Are you certain?"

"You are beautiful, but no."

The Queen sighed then turned to me. "It's better to be feared than loved anyway. Bandersnatch, seems you have a loyal man. Now you know," she said then grinned at me.

She picked up her robe and slid it back on. "That's what your boss wanted," she said, motioning to the small case she'd handed to William. "See them out," she added, motioning to henchman who opened the door.

He motioned for us to follow him.

More than happy to get out of there, I headed toward the door.

"My—Your Highness, if you don't mind, I wanted to ask about Anna. Are you…are you done with her?" I looked back to see William staring at the Queen.

"Anna?" the Queen replied, looking confused for a moment. "Oh yes, Miss Farm Fresh. I'm afraid she's quite dried up."

"If you've no use for her, maybe—"

"Take her. Consider it a bonus," she replied then sat down on the box the automatons had delivered. She rapped on the lid. "Comfy, love?" she called with a laugh.

William turned and nodded to me. We quickly headed out the door before the Queen could change her mind. I raced down the hallway to the room where I'd seen Anna. She lay on the floor.

I knelt down. "Anna?" I reached out and turned her face toward me.

Her eyes were wide open, frozen in the grimace of death.

"Too late," I whispered.

"Anna?" William said, kneeling beside me. He lifted her hand, feeling her wrist for any sign of life. He shook his head.

"Do you still want her?" the Queen's henchman asked, a sick joking tone in his voice.

William rose, glared at the man, then we turned and left, both our hearts sick with guilt.

As we walked back to London that night, I'd sworn it was the last time I would ever deal with the Queen of Hearts.

Apparently, I was wrong.

THE SUNLIGHT SHIMMERED THROUGH THE window onto William's dark hair. Tints of blue, gold, and copper shimmered in the sunlight.

I stared at him.

"Alice, I'm going to get out. I'm ending it. All of it. I can't live without you. I've saved as much as I can. You can't—won't—come back, and I don't blame you. So, I'm coming to you, as I promised. I just need to clean up this last problem." He reached out and touched my cheek. After a moment's thought, he leaned toward me.

I didn't pull back. I couldn't. Every piece of me had wanted this moment since the day I'd left.

He pulled me into a deep kiss. I smelled the scent of jasmine on his skin, the salty sweet taste of his mouth, the feel of his beard on my chin. And most of all, I felt the soul of the man I had never stopped loving. I kissed him deeply, falling into his embrace.

I had missed him terribly.

After several moments had passed, he pulled back then set his forehead against mine.

"I love you, Alice," he whispered. "I never stopped loving you."

"I love you too," I replied. "Now, let's steal that bloody diamond."

16
A GIRL'S BEST FRIEND

LATER THAT EVENING, WILLIAM AND I returned to Hyde Park. Merchant tents selling memorabilia and cheap replicas of the wonders inside were closed for the night. The taverns and betting places, including The Mushroom's temporary tented home on the green, were still alive with noise and action. William and I left The Mushroom and headed to the green space between the Crystal Palace and the vendors. We settled onto a park bench far enough away from the exhibition to avoid provoking attention but close enough for a good look. Constables cased the place, shooing off onlookers trying to peer within. Inside the actual exhibition, which was now closed, guards patrolled the halls.

Lifting a spyglass, I scanned the building. "There. On the exterior of the building. Just near the German exhibit. There is a ladder that reaches from the second to the third floor." I handed the spyglass to William.

He gazed at the ladder. "There are steel support beams. They look wide enough to move across if we're careful and keep our steps light. That section will be shadowed in the dark of night."

"We can't break the glass to get in. It will make too much noise."

William nodded. "Did you notice that the ceiling panels above the trees were cranked open to let the heat out?" He panned the spyglass toward the trees. "The tree limbs bend toward the open panels, but they're too slim to support any weight."

"Climb down the trees?" I asked, considering. "Might make too much noise. We need to slip down a rope. Quick and silent. Problem is, once we get the diamond, how do we get back out quickly? As soon as they realize the diamond is missing, they'll turn that place inside out," I said.

"Climb back up?"

I frowned. "Too high, and I'm too slow."

"We could try the trees on the way out."

"They'll think to search there if they're any good."

William raised an eyebrow at me. "When have they ever been any good?"

I chuckled then considered the problem. "They will only get alarmed if they know the diamond is missing. What if we don't melt the bars? What if we swipe the diamond and replace it with a fake? The diamond is so lackluster. A simple hunk of cut glass would mimic it easily."

William rubbed his finger across his chin. "We'd need access to the safe. The guard's key opens it, but that safe came from Buckingham. No way to get a copy."

"Who needs a copy? We just need to lift the real key from the guard. We'll come in at night, grab the diamond, swap it out with a fake, and then toss the key—"

"But getting out of the exhibit is the problem either way," William said.

"What if we stay the night? We do the job near dawn. The guards will be tired by then. That will be to our advantage. We could swipe the diamond then hide in one of the exhibits."

"Crawl inside a sarcophagus?" William asked with a grin.

"There are a million places to hide. When they open in the morning, we'd leave amongst the crowd," I suggested.

"Stay at the scene of the crime? I'm not sure—"

"What crime? Until the guard discovers his key is missing, there's nothing to worry about. We leave the key there, make it look like the guard dropped it. No one will be the wiser."

"Except we need to lift the key off the guard."

"Send Rabbit. His fingers are quick."

William nodded thoughtfully. "That could work."

"That could work."

"So, I need to track the guard who carries the key," William said.

"And I need a fake diamond."

"Take your pick," William said, motioning to the vendor tents behind us where the replicas were sold.

I stared at the building. It was a job just like any other job William and I had ever worked. But the risk here was very high. "If we get caught, we'll be sent to the Tower."

"The Queen of Hearts…there is no other way."

"I could talk to her, try to work out a deal."

"No," William said, shaking his head. "She's a sick woman. Don't go near her. I made a mistake. I didn't mean to, but it's done. Don't get any ideas in your mind, Alice. Stay away from her."

I frowned. "All right."

In the distance, the clock on Tinker's Tower sounded. It was already eleven o'clock.

"I need to go. I've already given Bess too much to worry about this week."

"I'll have the key by dusk tomorrow."

We both rose. It was a moonless night. Only the lights from the exhibition cast their shadowed glow on us.

"We can do this," William whispered. "Hell, if anything goes wrong, we'll just shoot our way out. It's a building made of glass, after all."

I laughed. "We can do this. It's just a snatch and run. Nothing new."

William chuckled then tapped me lightly on my nose. "Bandit."

I winked at him.

He leaned in and kissed me softly, first on the lips and then on the cheek. "Goodnight."

"Goodnight," I whispered, setting my hand on his cheek. I turned and headed back toward the city. The plan would work. It wasn't without risk, of course, but no job ever was. It may have been awhile since I'd stolen anything, but the job was part of me—for better or worse. Jabberwocky had trained his little apprentice very well.

But still, we were robbing our rightful Queen to pass over a treasure to a madwoman. Why? It was high time I found out.

17
WHAT THE KNAVE KNEW

THE HUSTLE WOULD STILL BE the same. The Knave would begin making the rounds at around ten, stopping by all the opium dens and pubs, playing a few hands of cards to line his own pockets before collecting William's cut. He'd finish his rounds by one o'clock then head home. He'd keep the money with him then drop it off at The Mushroom in the morning.

I left the lawn of the Crystal Palace and moved down the foggy cobblestone streets, seeking to stay unseen. I had no business skulking around in the dark. My life wasn't supposed to be like this anymore. I'd spent most of the last year pretending I didn't love William, but it was a lie. More than anything, I wanted to be with him. I just didn't want this…this mess, this blood. I would do anything to help William earn his freedom.

Because the truth was, I'd taken mine without regard to how it would impact him. And I was sorry for it. But saving William meant I needed to know what I was saving him from. I'd ended last night harassing airship pirates. Tonight I was stalking thugs.

The Knave's flat on Fleet Street was about as well-protected as a henhouse in a fox farm. With a quick twist and jiggle, I unlocked the door and let myself inside. Locking the door behind me, I headed into

his sparse kitchen. I dug through his cupboard until I found some tea then set a kettle to boil. Working with the light of a single candle in the kitchen, I set out two teacups and some strawberry pastries I'd found in a bakery box and then waited. It was around one thirty when I heard the lock jiggle. I sat still and waited, listening to the sound of his footfalls.

Seeing the candlelight burning, I heard Jack's footsteps stop. A moment later, I heard the click of a revolver. Pistol extended, he turned the corner.

"Tea?" I asked.

"Jesus, Mary, and Joseph. I nearly shot you, Alice."

I rose and poured us both a cup of tea.

"What are you doing here?"

"Waiting for you."

"Why?"

"Just thought we'd have a little chat."

Jack dropped into the chair then looked over the table. "I was saving those tarts for breakfast."

"Well, it is morning," I said.

He shook his head then laughed.

"Sugar?"

"No. I'm tired, Alice. What is it?"

"Why is William indebted to the Queen of Hearts?"

"He botched a deal."

"I know that. What I don't know is why?" I rose and prepared the teacups, setting a cup in front of Jack.

"It's complicated."

"So I've been told," I said, rolling my eyes.

Jack picked up his teacup, blew across the hot liquid, then took a sip. "If he doesn't want you to know, there must be a reason."

"Perhaps. But it can't be a very good one. Jack, please. We've been friends since we were children. William is in trouble. I want to help him. I just need to know what happened."

"Why does it matter?"

"It matters."

"Do you still love him?"

"Would I be here if I didn't?"

Jack laughed. "You and William are like the sun and the moon, chasing and following one another in an endless loop. He still loves you as much as he did the day you left. And you wouldn't be here if you didn't love him."

"Indeed. So stop prattling."

Jack slid a plate with one of the pastries on it toward him. He lifted his fork and took a bite. "The Queen of Hearts wanted some unusual merchandise," he said between bites. "William procured it for her. Now, mind you, he didn't know what he was procuring. William was the go-between. We passed letters, made the arrangements, traded money. But when the merchandise arrived in London. Well, William couldn't go through with it. And I didn't blame him."

"Why? What was the product?"

Jack wouldn't meet my eye.

"You're avoiding my question. What was the merchandise?"

Jack exhaled deeply. "Girls."

"Girls?"

"Young girls. They were just kids. I don't know where they came from. The captain of the *Medusa* brought them in," Jack said then shook his head. "I saw them myself. It was…it was awful. William took one look at those girls and everything was over. I don't know where those girls went. William called in a favor with an airship jockey Jabberwocky used to work with. Lady captain. Pilots the *Aphrodite*. She took those girls out of London. I don't know where they went, but I do know they didn't go to the Queen of Hearts. That was the deal that went bad. That's why he's on the hook with the Queen."

I didn't understand. Certainly, the Queen's perversions were growing even sicker, but there was something more at play here. I rose and set my hand on Jack's shoulder. "Thank you."

Jack shook his head. "This is bloody business. She's going to have his head if he doesn't come up with either those girls or that diamond."

"Do you know why?"

Jack shook his head. "No. But the Countess is somehow involved. I blame Jabberwocky. William was trying to clean up the last of his obligations."

I frowned. Now, why would the Countess be involved? But then I remembered the night I'd seen the Queen of Hearts in her wretched bath. The Countess had been there. Had I been wrong to trust her? She and Jabberwocky had been lovers. I knew her ever since I was a child. She'd always treated Bess and me in the most loving of ways. Something was just wrong here. "Then it's time to end it. For all our sakes."

Jack nodded. "Thanks for the tea," he said, lifting his cup. "Not a bad thing having a woman waiting at home for you. You know—" he said, a mischievous glint in his eyes.

I smirked and shook my head. I headed to the door. "Good night, Jack."

"'Night, Alice," he said with a smile.

I closed the door to Jack's flat then headed outside. Before I exited back onto the street, I stopped and leaned against the wall. I squinted my eyes shut. Flashes of the Queen in all her bloody glory appeared before my eyes. Young girls? Why had she wanted young girls? Many dark answers came to mind. I was proud of William that he had done what was right, but at what cost to him?

Even if we did get the diamond, then what?

The Queen of Hearts, in all her madness, would carry on. Shouldn't she be stopped? If she was seeking young girls, with sanguine or other reasons in mind, then someone should intervene—permanently.

I could snatch the diamond. That had never been a concern. But maybe that wasn't the best solution. Maybe there was another way out of this.

I could kill the Queen of Hearts.

18

SISTERS & MISTERS

I ENTERED THE FLAT QUIETLY so as not to wake Bess. I was surprised to see her sitting at our small kitchen table. She was painting a teacup by the light of a single candle.

She didn't say a word when I entered, just smiled at me then set down the cup she'd been painting. She rose and went to the fireplace from which she retrieved a bowl that had been sitting by the fire. She uncovered it, revealing the steaming hot stew inside then set it on the table. She laid out a spoon then poured me an ale. She motioned for me to sit.

"How was it? The Crystal Palace?" I asked carefully.

She smiled serenely then turned the teacup so I could see what she had been painting. "Look," she said, motioning to her drying rack where a dozen other small vases, cups, and plates were sitting. They had been painted with brilliant blue and white flowers, just like the Chinese vases. "I've been painting since we returned. I couldn't get the images out of my mind."

"The visit wasn't too taxing?"

"Oh no. Not at all. Henry took great care to make sure I rested frequently. It was truly a wonderland. Never in my wildest dreams could I imagine such a place. I loved the hand-painted silks from Japan. Did you see them?"

I shook my head then sipped the ale.

Bess sighed happily as she looked over her handiwork. "They're turning out nicely, I think."

"Truly lovely. Bess, I'm sorry if you—"

I began but Bess raised her hand to stop me. "Henry...he told me everything. He told me about the trouble he got himself into and how you got him out of it."

I raised an eyebrow at her. "Then why do you look so happy?"

She laughed. "The question is, why do *you* look so happy?" She set her teacup down and dropped her paintbrush into a jar of water. "You haven't been happy since the day we left. We are free, and our life has been honest, but at what cost? These last three days, I've seen a light inside of you that I haven't seen in a very long time. And it's not the job. You've finally remembered."

"Remembered what?"

"That you love William."

"I…I thought I was over him."

Bess laughed. "You don't just get over the love of your life."

"He's trying to get out. He has one last problem to solve, and then we can make a new future, all of us," I told her. My words came out sounding more like an excuse than I meant them too.

Bess shrugged lightly. "Whatever needs to be done, that's what will be done," she said then picked up her brush once more.

A moment later, I felt something rub against my shin. I looked down expecting to find Dinah, but it was the clockwork cat looking up at me expectantly.

"Designed to beg for scraps, are you? No nuts, bolts, or oil here, I'm afraid," I said, patting my Cheshire cat on his metal head.

The cat meowed then crossed the room. It jumped up onto my small cot, turning until it found a comfortable position, then lay down. It looked out at me with its wide aquamarine-colored eyes then smiled.

Bess laughed. "How's the stew? I tried to keep it warm for you."

"It's perfect."

"You know, I've missed William," she said. "Tell him I want him to come by. I want to thank him for the tickets."

I smiled at her. "I'll tell him tomorrow."

Bess raised an eyebrow at me. "Tomorrow? Very good. I hope it all goes as you wish."

I smiled but didn't reply.

That made two of us.

19
A RAVEN AND A WRITING DESK

THE NEXT MORNING, I ROSE early and got dressed while Bess slept. She coughed a few times in her sleep. Her breaths carried a sharp wheeze I didn't like. I lifted the amber bottle of syrup on the counter to discover there was barely a dose left. I would need to go to the apothecary before I did anything else.

I slipped on a pair of tan trousers, a dark blue shirt, and a leather corset. I slid the White Queen into my boot, pulled on my coat, then headed outside.

The morning air was crisp. A steam-powered machine rolled down the cobblestone street, causing everyone to move aside. A massive cloud billowed around it.

The apothecary's shop was at the end of the lane. Through the window, I could see Mister Arnold was already hard at work. I pushed the door open to the little shop. A tiny bell overhead jangled. The tangy scents of the medicines assailed my nose. The walls of the apothecary were lined with glass jars filled with a variety of herbs. White porcelain containers held powders and other oddities.

"Good morning, Alice," Mister Arnold said. He was a slight man, the majority of his weight coming from the mass of curly white ringlets on his head. He was staring down at the table in front of him. The optics he wore magnified his vision. His eyes looked ten times their size.

"What are you looking at?" I asked.

"A dried extract of lemon. It's proving useful in the treatment of scurvy," he said then pulled off the optics. "How is Bess?"

"Cough is still rattling. She needs more syrup."

Mister Arnold nodded then went to his cupboards. "I have something new I want your sister to try. It's a salve. I met a very bright apothecary from Scotland a few weeks back. He told me it's effective for patients like your sister. She should rub the salve on her chest at night. It should ease her breathing."

I opened my coin purse and looked inside. An impromptu airship ride to Twickenham had pushed my weekly budget to its limit. When I looked inside, I saw that if Bess and I wanted to eat this week, an additional purchase of medicine was out of the question. "I'm afraid it will have to wait until my next payment."

Mister Arnold nodded sympathetically. "Let's do this. We'll just try it this week, an experiment on my part, and if her condition improves, we'll work out a payment schedule."

Mister Arnold had always been very kind to Bess and me. There was something about Bess' nature that always brought out the best in people. Even when we'd lived in the workhouse, Bess's sweetness had earned her the affection of Mister Townsend who didn't push her as hard as the others given her fragile condition. That sweetness lingered wherever my sister went.

"Thank you, sir."

"Just let me know how it works. This time of year is terrible for people with hay fever and a rattle like your sister has."

"I will. Thank you so much."

Mister Arnold slipped the syrup and a small jar of salve into a bag. He jotted down some instructions on a piece of paper and added that as well. He handed the bag to me. "Not in uniform today?"

"No, my employer went to the countryside. I have the rest of the week off."

"Get some rest then, my dear. You look tired. I believe you work too hard, Miss Lewis."

"We all do what we must. Thank you again," I said, motioning to the bag, then headed outside.

Bag in hand, I headed down the street in the direction of Henry's millinery shop.

Despite the blessings bestowed upon us through the kindness of others, at times I hated how poor Bess and I had become. Of course, we'd been born into a poor life. Even when our parents were alive, our life had been that of paupers. I remembered very little now. The four of us had lived above a perfumer's shop in South Hampton. I remembered watching the well-dressed ladies and gentlemen filing in and out of the boutique, purchasing single bottles that cost more than, I would guess, what my parents made in a month. When a fierce winter sickness had passed through one year when I was about seven, Bess six, both our parents had perished. Bess was left with a rattle that never left her chest. Only I had escaped the ailment unscathed. With no better recourse available to two orphans, we'd ended up at Mister Townsend's workhouse. But fate had seen a different course for us. We were there barely two years before chance threw Mister Mock—Jabberwocky—into our path.

As I walked toward Henry's shop, I realized that, in truth, my current poverty was entirely my own fault. I did have a life of comfort. Under Jabberwocky's care, Bess and I had lived well. But we'd left that life of our own accord. My reasons for leaving were good. I was no killer. I could not live with the blood on my hands, and I never wanted to risk it again. But had I really needed to leave? Did I really have to banish Bess and me to a poor but honest life? I was unsure. I'd tried not to think about how it all had ended. But now, with William in my life once more, everything I had given up smacked me in the face. I had given up more than just a life of crime. Bess was right. I had given up my true love. The memory of our last day at Jabberwocky's house, and my fight with William, was still fresh in my memory.

"ALICE," WILLIAM SAID ONCE MORE, "please reconsider." He was standing in the doorway of my room in Jabberwocky's house as I packed up the last of my clothes.

Everything had unfolded so quickly. William had stepped into Jabberwocky's place without any obstacles. Once it was clear to the others I would not take over, it was only natural that William would do the job. Jabberwocky was dead. My hands were still stained with blood that only I could see. Every time I closed my eyes, the image of the banker's face, mouth open wide, eyes bulging, came to mind. When I paired such images with the Queen of Hearts's bloody bath, the endless array of naked tarts I had to look at every time I entered The Mushroom, the airship pirates and crooked dealers, I just didn't want it. Just because a grown man had taught a little girl to steal, and because she'd been good at it, didn't mean it was a life for which she'd been destined.

"Why don't *you* reconsider," I replied. "Leave with us. Let Jack or someone else do the job. We don't have to live like this."

"Alice, you're being rash. This is your home. Even if you don't want work, at least stay here. You wouldn't have to do another job again. You can be done with it."

"And do what to earn my keep?" I asked angrily as I shoved a pair of trousers into my bag.

"Nothing. Marry me, Alice. Stay here. Be my wife."

I turned and looked at him, my eyes wide. "I can't quite tell, are you proposing to me or yelling at me?"

"Both," he said, then smiled softly. He crossed the room and took my hands. "Don't go. I love you."

"I love you too. I just...I can't get past what happened with the banker."

"Nothing like that will ever touch you again. You won't see it. Won't be part of it."

"But you will. And it will come home with you every day."

"What would you have me do, become a groom, a tailor? Jabberwocky trained me for this life. I don't know how to do anything else."

"There are people who can help us."

"Like the Countess? I understand she is looking for a position for you."

"She can help you too."

"Shall I go from being master of this house to being some rich man's butler?"

"From a life as a thief and killer to that of an honest man."

"I've never killed anyone."

"Isn't that convenient."

"I don't mean it like that."

"This is not a life I ever wanted."

"Then you are saying no."

"To staying here? To staying in the life? I am saying no."

"And what are you saying to me? What is your answer for me?" he whispered, then brushed my hair away from my face. "Alice Lewis, I've been in love with you from the moment I set eyes on you. Marry me."

"Leave with me."

"I can't."

"Then my answer has to be no."

"But Alice—"

"I love you, William. I love you more than anything. I love you enough that I killed to protect you. You will never find anyone who cares for you as I do. But I can't stay in this life. I made a promise to Bess long ago that when Jabberwocky was gone, we'd leave. She cannot handle all this darkness. We must get away. Please come with us. We could travel. See the world. Isn't that something you have always wanted? *You*, not what Jabberwocky made you into, something *you* wanted? We could go somewhere warm where Bess's health will improve. What about Barbados? Or maybe Tahiti? Let's leave this place and start somewhere new."

"People are depending on me now. I can't just let everything Jabberwocky worked so hard for fall into pieces."

"Then settle his affairs and join me. Settle his affairs and be done with it."

"I…I don't know."

I closed the case and took it by the handle. "My carriage is downstairs. I'm going. If you choose this life, choose it all the way. I don't want any part of it. Do you understand? If you choose this life, you choose it in total. Don't bother me or mine until you have something worth saying."

"'I love you' is not enough? 'Be my wife' is not enough?"

I looked him deeply in the eyes. "I love you too," I whispered then leaned in and kissed him. I let my lips linger long on his. I caught his scent and the sweet taste of vanilla on his lips, and then I stepped back. "When you're ready to choose me, and only me, you'll be able to find me. Until then, I have to say goodbye."

I turned and left William standing there.

And I didn't look back.

I STOPPED IN THE MIDDLE of the street and wiped away the tear slipping down my cheek. I had been foolish and rash. At the time, I wasn't thinking clearly. I could have helped William settle Jabberwocky's affairs and gotten us both out. The banker's death had split me down the middle. Followed by the scene with the Queen of Hearts and Jabberwocky's death, and I hadn't been thinking straight. The horrible realization racked me. I had been wrong. All this time, I was the one who was wrong. I'd left a man who'd loved me enough to marry me. And I still loved him. I had done wrong by him when I'd left. Now I had a chance to make it right. No matter what, I would get him out of this debt to the Queen of Hearts.

I slowed as I reached Henry's shop. The front window boasted a beautiful display of hats. I paused a moment to gaze at them—after I managed to find a spot amongst the women already gathered there. There was a gorgeous pink and green silk top hat trimmed with flowers. What made the hat unique, however, was the clockwork butterfly whose copper wings wagged gently as it floated all around the hat, fluttering from flower to flower. If you looked hard enough, you could see it was attached to the hat with the thinnest piece of wire. Another top hat depicted a skyline view of London. A little metal airship, a replica of the famous airship *Stargazer*, piloted by the renowned airship racer Lily Stargazer, made its trek around the circumference of the hat over and over again. There was also a hat that featured a replica of the Tinker's Tower. The face had a working clock. I looked beyond the clever creations and saw Henry at his workbench inside. I went in.

"Alice?" Henry said, standing. His brow furrowed with worry. "Is everything all right?"

I nodded. "I have an errand to run. I stopped by the apothecary. Would you mind taking this to Bess when you go for lunch?" I asked, holding out the bag.

"Of course. She's out of medicine already?"

I nodded.

A troubled expression crossed Henry's face, but he didn't say anything. There was no need. Worrying about Bess was a state in which Henry and I both lived.

"So, were the tea service hats well received?" I asked, sitting down across from Henry.

He laughed. "Oh yes. And the chief conspirator, Mrs. Wolston, ordered something new in celebration of the Grand Exhibition," he said then pulled a hat off a box sitting nearby.

I laughed out loud when I saw it. The base of the hat was made with white silk, but the top of the hat was made to resemble the same arched beams and glass of the Crystal Palace.

"I'm still working on the faux glass insets. We'll use spun sugar for the glass."

"It won't melt?"

He shook his head. "I'll just have to warn her not to get her hair too close. She won't want it to stick."

I laughed.

"Around the brim, I'm trimming it with the delights of the exhibition. Look," he said, lifting a small wooden boat with a paper sail, an exact replica from the India display. Beside it, he set a miniature Colt, the pistol that had been on display in the American exhibit.

"Does it work?" I asked, picking up the tiny gun.

"Well, I'm no gunsmith, but I do appreciate realism," he replied. He motioned toward a hatbox nearby.

Taking aim, I squeezed the tiny trigger with the tip of my fingernail. The little gun made a louder bang than I expected.

I laughed.

"I'm working on a clockwork cat today," he said, pointing to a small box of metal bits sitting on the table. "Your Chess is my model. I'll create his likeness with watch parts. Your miniature feline will be ticking in no time.

"Alice, I have something I must confess," Henry said, his voice turning serious.

I was looking into the box from which Henry had pulled the hat. Inside I saw miniature versions of taxidermied elephants, samurai suits, a tiny Chinese vase—on which I saw Bess's handiwork—a miniature velocipede, but then one item caught my eye. I reached into the box and pulled out an exact replica of the Koh-i-Noor. Steadying it on the palm of my hand, I studied it in the light of the lamp sitting on the table.

"Alice? Did you hear me?" Henry asked.

"Yes. Henry, where did you get this?"

"Did you see the real thing? Muddy hunk of diamond, wasn't it?" Henry said as he fingered through the clockwork parts. "I couldn't sleep last night, so I spent the whole night trying to get the cut on the replica perfect," he said, motioning to a pamphlet on the diamond he must have gotten from the exhibition. The pamphlet showed the exact proportions of the diamond. "I was going to use a crystal to give it more sparkle, but the real stone is too dim. So, I went with dim for the realism. My grandfather—did you know he was a jewelry maker?—had an old stone someone had given to him in payment. Not a diamond, not a crystal, not even a topaz, just some odd gem attached to a hunk of limestone. My grandfather never did anything to it. Since neither my father nor I followed him into the trade, that old rock has just been sitting in a box all this time. Turns out, it was perfect. Large enough, and dull enough, to make a perfect replica. But Alice, I really must tell you—"

"Yes, I know. You told Bess. Henry," I gasped. I wrapped my hand tightly around the gem and squeezed my eyes shut.

"Alice, what is it?"

I opened my eyes and stared at him. "Are you sure it's a perfect match? You're absolutely certain?"

"Yes. Same weight. Same cut. Same lifeless sparkle."

"Can I have it?"

"Have it? Why?"

I opened my mouth twice, trying to find a way to explain. Henry stared at me. The more at a loss for words I was, the more the blood began to drain from his face.

"Alice," he whispered, aghast, "what have I gotten you into?"

I shook my head. "Not me. William. I need this stone. Are you sure it's exact? Are you sure no one could tell the difference? A gem expert? A jeweler? Are you certain?"

Henry stared at me, his eyes wide. "Alice?"

"Are you certain?"

"Yes, I'm certain. I apprenticed under my grandfather. I know everything there is to know about gems. I just didn't like working with metals. Silk was always easier on the hands. It's exact."

Leaning across the table, I wrapped my arms around Henry and hugged him hard.

"Alice?"

"I'm sorry. I have to have it. I have to. And you must never tell anyone anything about it."

"All right. But Alice—"

"You promise?"

"Yes."

"This makes us even," I said, pinching his cheek playfully.

He smiled nervously. "I don't know what you're into, Alice. But I have a feeling I just saved you from a big mistake."

"I hope so. I need to go now," I said, gathering myself together.

"Be careful."

He was right. It was a good fake. A perfect fake. But it was still a fake, which meant there was risk involved, for everyone.

I looked back at Henry. "When you make the new replica for the hat, don't be perfect. Make sure the cut isn't right and that the gem sparkles too much."

"Why?"

"To ensure that no one ever suspects you can do better."

Understanding, Henry nodded.

I looked down at the gem in my hand. It really did look exactly like the diamond. "Any more of this stone left?" I asked him.

He raised an eyebrow at me then nodded.

"Good. Then get to work."

"On what?"

"On an engagement ring for my sister," I said with a smile, and then turned and left.

20
WHAT THE COUNTESS KNEW

WHEN I REACHED THE MUSHROOM, I was not surprised to find the Countess's auto sitting outside. It had been a year since I'd been inside Jabberwocky's old pub—at least its more permanent residence. The makeshift tent on the Hyde Park green was already enough of a reminder of the life I'd left behind. The pub had practically been a second home to me and all the others Jabberwocky had adopted into the life.

The scene inside the pub was sleepy. The lights were dim, but the familiar smell of alcohol hung heavy in the air. A few patrons sat huddled at tables, hovering over their drinks as they spoke in low tones. I spotted a weapons dealer I knew. They called him Lobster on account of his hand being frozen into an awkward claw after one of his products had detonated in his hand.

At first, he passed me a cursory glance. Recognizing me, he nodded. I'd worked jobs for him at least twice, lifting some hard-to-find parts. At the back of the pub, William's guards eyed me skeptically. One of then went into the back office. A few moments later, Jack appeared.

"Morning, Alice. Want tea?"

I shook my head. "Is the Countess in the back?"

He nodded then waved for me to follow him.

Jabberwocky's old office—now William's—looked much the same. Nothing had changed besides the man sitting behind the desk. I noticed that William had even left hanging the painting of Madame Mock which Bess had painted as a gift to Jabberwocky.

The Countess was sitting in a chair across from William sipping on a glass of some amber-colored liquid. She stopped midsentence when I entered.

"Alice," she said nicely.

With a nod to William, Jack closed the door then left.

"I got your message," the Countess said.

I turned to William. "I'd inquired of the Countess as to why the Queen wanted the diamond. It seemed an extreme acquisition, and I suspected the Countess might have some additional information," I said, looking at her sharply.

The Countess nodded, a guilty expression passing over her features. "Please understand, I had no idea she would pull the two of you into this.

If I had known, I would have done my best to forestall her."

"Jabberwocky...I took the job to pay off the last of Jabberwocky's debt to her," William explained.

The Countess frowned. "Then I am twice at fault."

William and I both looked at her.

"The Queen of Hearts sought, some years back, to expose me if I didn't help her. Jabberwocky helped me buy her silence," the Countess explained.

"You said she threatened to expose you. Expose what?" I asked.

"My dear, what do you think the gentry would make of an occultist in their mix? It's one thing to do favors for certain high-up people who want those favors kept secret. It's quite another matter when those secrets are exposed."

"She was blackmailing you."

"Yes. Jabberwocky did jobs for her to keep her silent...and so did I."

"I remember. You were there the night she was in that bathtub filled with blood," I said.

The Countess swirled the liquid in her cup. "For years, the Queen of Hearts has found my Uncle Horace's collection of books—and my skills by extension—curious. She's been looking for something. Her interest in the dark arts, as I believe the two of you already know, is deeply personal."

"Yes," I nodded, shuddering to think of the night I'd seen her consume Anna's living blood.

"In exchange for her silence, the Queen has had me working to help her acquire certain knowledge. It began with a book she traced to Uncle

Horace's collection. That book chronicled the enchantments used by a Hungarian Countess by the name of Elizabeth Bathory."

"Why? What information is she hunting?" William asked.

The Countess took a swig of her drink. "She's looking for ways to stay young. She's seeking the path to immortality. Bathory believed that bathing in the blood of virgins could extend one's youth."

"That's madness," William said.

"Is it?" The Countess replied. "When I first met the Queen, she and I were the same age."

We both stared at her. But she was right. I had seen it myself.

"So she's seeking spells, elixirs," William said.

"More than that, but I have managed to keep such knowledge—what I know of it, at least—hidden from her. She would go the way of Faust and summon up a demon if she could."

William laughed nervously. "But such knowledge…that's impossible."

The Countess raised an eyebrow and the expression on her face told me it was, in fact, very possible. I shuddered at the thought. "Some time ago my late husband—with whom I had a very contentious relationship— sold many of the books in Uncle Horace's collection just to spite me. May you rot in hell," she said, looking at the ground. "The Queen acquired a volume from that collection which contained a spell written by an Egyptian priest. The book was annotated, half translated, and appeared to have the ritual the Queen was after."

"What kind of spell?" I asked.

"One that grants immortality. Of course, you had to have the right ingredients to make it work. And that is where her royal highness of insanity ran into some problems. I take it the deal you botched involved the acquisition of some of those...ingredients?" the Countess asked, turning to William.

"I...I'm not sure."

She smiled carefully at him, an expression that told us both that she already knew the answer. "Well, no matter. She found a way. The task she set you on, William, and Alice by inadvertent extension, was to pluck another important element needed for the ritual. She needs a blood diamond."

"A blood diamond?" William asked.

"A diamond that has caused many deaths," the Countess explained. "The bloodier the diamond, the better. And what bloodier diamond is there than the Koh-i-Noor? Of course, the diamond is not the only thing she needed. She also needed a complete translation of the ritual, which I now have. So, now, I have the words, and she has everything else she needs except the diamond. Once she has that, the potion can be prepared and the ritual completed."

"A potion? You mean, something she will drink?" William asked.

The Countess nodded.

"Will it work?" I asked, aghast.

The Countess shrugged. "I have no idea. But I know that this is where

Anastasia Otranto and I will part ways. This is the last debt I owe her."

"You're not the only one," William mumbled.

"Anastasia Otranto…why do I know that name?" I asked.

"The banker," William replied. "That was the name on the paperwork the banker had. We botched the job, Alice. We missed something in the banker's vault. That's why…that's why I was doing one last job for her, to clear off our—Jabberwocky's—mistake."

I frowned. "Anastasia Otranto. Who—"

"That, my dears, is the Queen of Hearts's real name," the Countess interjected.

William and I stared at one another.

"So, you're planning to do the job?" the Countess asked. "Get the diamond? The Queen was quite adamant that it was the only way she'd release you from Jabberwocky's debt."

"Tonight," William said.

"I'll be visiting her today with the rest of the translation. She's invited me for a game of—"

I reached into my pocket, pulled out the gem, and set it on William's desk.

The Countess stopped midspeech.

William rose.

For several long minutes, no one spoke.

"Alice," William finally whispered.

"I went back last night. I went in through the roof, just as we planned.

Down the rope. Dodged the guards. The lock wasn't that difficult to pick. In and out. Snatched. Just like always."

"What about the gem on display? What did you—"

"I lifted a fake from one of the souvenir tents on the green. Swapped it with the real one."

"They'll figure it out. They'll notice," William said.

"Eventually. But the fake looked good to the eye."

The Countess picked up the gem and looked at it. She studied it closely then set it back down. "It doesn't *feel* cursed."

"It isn't, at least not to us. Only cursed for male British monarchs, right?" I replied.

William nodded. "I need to send word to Rabbit. He was going to trail the guard. I need to call him off."

I nodded to him.

William rose and left the office, leaving me and the Countess alone.

"This potion. If any of the ingredients are not exact, what will happen?"

The Countess raised an eyebrow at me then shrugged. "Perhaps nothing. Perhaps she'll get a stomach ache. Perhaps she'll have a fit and lop off everyone's heads. Or..."

"Or?"

"Or, it will kill her." The Countess picked up the gem once more. She studied it closely. She then wrapped her hands around it and closed her eyes. A strange expression crossed her face, and for a moment, I'd swear

I saw white light emanating from her clenched hand. After a moment, she relaxed once more and studied the diamond closely. "You know, Jabberwocky always told me you were the most intelligent child he'd ever met. From the moment he saw you, he knew you were special. You are. This diamond is exact. But this stone is not cursed."

"Of course it is," I said with a smirk.

"It's a risk, Bandersnatch. She'll have someone there to check the gem."

I shrugged. "Do you think a gem master will be able to sense whether it is cursed or not? Seems like something only someone gifted in the occult would notice."

The Countess smirked, shook her head, and then handed the gem back to me.

"So, you're planning to visit the Queen today? Mind if we come along?"

The Countess lifted her glass, polishing it off, then set the cup back down. "Do you play croquet?" she asked with a grin.

21
OF WICKETS, FLAMINGOS, AND RANDOM BEHEADINGS

THE COUNTESS SLIPPED INTO THE driver's seat of her auto, motioning for me to take the seat beside her. William and Jack—who we'd brought along for muscle—slid into the back passenger seat.

My heart was pounding. If the Queen discovered the stone was a fake, she'd be out for blood. But I took Henry's word as truth. She wouldn't be able to tell the difference.

I had debated whether or not to tell William the diamond was a sham. But the moment I saw him sitting in Jabberwocky's chair, I knew I should lie. If the deal went bad, it would be on me and me alone. I had left William to clean up Jabberwocky's debts, and I'd been wrong. William was in this situation now, in part because of me. He wasn't dragging me back into anything. He could have walked away when I did, but he'd felt obligated to Jabberwocky in a way I hadn't. I didn't see that then, but I understood now. For the last year, the man I'd loved was trying to find his way back to me. The tremendous realization hit me hard, and I was overwhelmed with a sense of guilt. I owed him.

The countess swerved around carriages, startling the horses, as she sped down the narrow streets. I'd sworn to myself I'd never step foot in the Queen of Hearts's abbey again. I was wrong. When we pulled up to the abbey's gate, the guards let the Countess through with a wave. She pulled her auto to a stop, parking it alongside the carriages and an odd cart with motorized wheels that reeked of algae.

With the Countess taking the lead, we headed toward the front door.

A tall man with very pale skin and a vacant look in his eyes met us there. "Around the back, please."

The flagstones of the path leading to the back of the house were arranged in a black and white brick pattern which resembled a chessboard. We passed under a wrought-iron arch into an elaborate rose garden. Bright red roses were in full bloom. Strange, of course, since they were out of season. Even more curious was that, despite the fact that the roses were so lovely, two of the Queen's automatons were going from bush to bush sprinkling a powder on the blossoms. I slowed to watch as we passed. As the powder landed on the blooms, their pigment faded. They turned white.

"Well, that's an odd sight," Jack whispered.

"Nothing compared to what we'll find next, no doubt," William replied.

We passed through the rose garden toward the large grassy area where several other people milled about. An odd ensemble of people was gathered there. One group included an older man and woman and half a dozen young girls from, presumably, Japan. They were dressed in fine silk robes, their dark hair held up with sticks. They giggled excitedly as they watched the automatons recolor the roses. I scanned the crowd, recognizing a French smuggler who frequented The Mushroom. He spotted us as well. He nodded to William.

"Beaumont," Jack whispered.

William nodded.

"Countess Waldegrave," a very round man called. His wife, who looked exceedingly bored, barely cast a glance our way.

The Countess nodded and crossed the grass to meet him.

"Mallet," a footman said, holding a croquet mallet toward me.

"We're here on business," I told him.

"Take a mallet."

Each of us took one of the wooden mallets, and then we waited.

There was a flurry of action at the back of the house, and then a very odd looking group appeared. A man at the front pushed a cart loaded down with something pink and fluffy. Behind him walked several young women, all of whom looked very pale and thin. They each wore thin gowns that looked like little more than chemises. Behind them were several guards, and at last came the Queen and her favorite henchman. Alongside the Queen, however, walked a very tall and handsome man. He was dressed in a fine suit and had a mop of black curls and striking blue eyes. In fact, they were so striking that when I studied them more closely, I realized they were not eyes at all. They were optics. The man had a very large wound across his neck that seemed to have been sewn shut in a haphazard manner, and his left arm appeared to be entirely mechanical. His clockwork hand glinted in the sunlight, offsetting his dreadfully pale skin. Despite his unusual appearance, he was doting on the Queen of Hearts who walked at his side.

Dressed in a long black gown and wearing a large black hat, its veil open at the front, she looked like she was no older than a girl of sixteen. Her flawless skin made her appear as if she'd been carved from marble. I couldn't help but stare.

"Do you see what I see?" William whispered.

I nodded.

The Queen sat down in a tall-backed wicker chair, the handsome—and possibly undead—man sitting beside her. Two of the Queen's girls sat at her feet. The rest of us stirred nervously. Only the Japanese visitors seemed unaware of the danger they were in. The Queen looked over the crowd. She paused when her gaze fell on William, Jack, and me.

"Well, I don't recall inviting you," she said.

The Countess left her portly friend and joined us. "I asked them to join me. They mentioned they had some business to transact. I happened to be on my way here. We thought it would make the day more festive if we all came out for croquet."

"Festive?" she replied with a snort. "Very well."

"First players," she called, motioning to the French smuggler, Beaumont. "Choose two players," she told him. The Queen motioned for her maidens and her henchman to join Beaumont and his companion for a game of croquet. The course was already set with a game of nine-wicket.

"Eh, Madame, we've no mallets," Beaumont said.

"Here you are. Select the best one. Some have a bit more give than the others," she said with a laugh which the handsome man beside her echoed. She waved to the cart.

Straining to look, I noticed then that on the cart was heaped with dead flamingos.

When the madness of the situation became clear, Beaumont's companion protested.

"Madame, this is ridiculous. How are we intended to play like this? We have business to discuss. This is a waste of—"

The Queen rose abruptly. "Off with his head," she screamed.

Before anyone could move, one of the nearby automatons turned and moved forward quickly. Swinging a massive ax, it lopped the Frenchman's head off. It bounced into the rose bushes. The body slumped over into the grass.

"Now look, you've made a mess. Take the body away," she told one her guards. The swift brutality of the scene racked me. This was the Queen of Hearts I remembered well. "Choose another player, and pick your mallet already," the Queen told Beaumont.

The man clenched his jaw hard then motioned to another of his comrades. He walked over to the cart and picked up a flamingo.

"The Queen had a shipment she was trying to deliver to Germany. Beaumont lost the merchandise to pirates," William whispered in my ear.

"Quiet," the Queen yelled in William's direction. "Begin," she called, turning to Beaumont once more.

At that, the Queen's maiden smacked her first ball and the game began.

We watched as the players worked their way around the yard. Beaumont, it seemed, was quite good. His flamingo apparently had a case of rigor mortis. When the final shots were made, Beaumont completed first. The henchman and the Queen's girl finished second and third, followed by Beaumont's surviving companion.

"You play well," the Queen told Beaumont.

"Oui, Madame. I played as a boy."

"Very good," she said then rose. "Kneel before me," she told Beaumont and his companion.

Frowning, Beaumont and his man knelt.

"Kiss my ring," she said, holding out her hand.

"But Madame, you're not wearing a ring," Beaumont protested.

"Are you calling me a liar?" she asked.

Beaumont stiffened. "Non, it's just that—"

"Off with their heads," she yelled, and before the men could move, another guard swept in and decapitated Beaumont and his man.

"Bloody hell," Jack exclaimed.

The bodies were dragged off. Two of the Queen's girls went to retrieve the heads. One of the girls brought Beaumont's head back to the Queen. She held the head, looking into his face, completely undisturbed by the fact that blood was leaking all over her dress.

"He's a handsome one, isn't he," she said to one of her girls, who merely smiled.

The Queen brought the head close to her and kissed his lips.

"Yuck," she protested. "Bad breath. Next game! Who wants to play next? You?" she asked the portly man.

"N-n-no, thank you," the man stammered nervously. Curiously, his wife yawned and looked around as if nothing off was happening. "I have what you wanted," he added in a loud whisper. He pointed to his coat pocket.

"Good," the Queen said pertly. "Take him and his *wife* inside," she told one of her girls.

"Oh, thank you. Thank you," the man replied. He pulled his unaware wife along behind him.

"Up for a game, Countess? Why don't you play my guests in the second field?" the Queen offered. In a garden row just beside ours, another game had already been set up.

The Countess motioned for the Japanese group—who looked like they were not sure if they should run, cry, or fight—to follow her.

"Now," the Queen said, turning her attention to us. "What to do with my unexpected guests."

"We also have some business to discuss," William told her.

Ignoring him, the Queen looked at me. "I haven't seen you in a while, Bandersnatch. Someone told me you were off the chess board."

"I was."

"Then why are you here?"

"I think you know why."

The Queen looked at William. "Couldn't pull off the job without your girl? I didn't think so. Must have been an awkward reunion."

William didn't say anything.

"Caterpillar. You're so serious," she said with a laugh then rose. "Alice, wasn't it? Let's have a match. You and the Knave against me and my girl."

When the Queen stepped beside me, she looked deep into my eyes. She was still the same dangerous woman…even if she now looked like she was my junior.

"Very well," I replied.

"Alice," Jack protested.

"He's afraid I'm going to behead him," the Queen said.

"Seems prudent."

"He and your Caterpillar did steal my tarts. Did you know?"

I looked back at William. The expression on his face told me he feared that I did, in fact, know the truth. "Yes."

William sucked in his lips and shook his head softly. Guilt stole over his face.

"Caterpillar wormed his way out of that one, made a new deal. Which is, of course, why I have the Bandersnatch in my house once more," she said then leaned in close. "Did you snatch what I was after?"

"Yes."

"Very good. Let's play."

The balls were lined up, and we began. William shifted nervously as we moved around the green.

"Got it! Beat that, Bandersnatch," the Queen yelled as her ball rolled through the wicket.

"Well done," I said through gritted teeth. I took aim with my mallet, knocking the ball through the wicket, but it rolled into the tall grass. We just needed to get through this. It was almost over. Very soon, we would all be free.

One of the Queen's girls, then Jack, took their shots after me. Once again, the Queen made a deft shot. I followed my ball into the grass and smacked it miserably back toward the green. The shot went wide, which made the Queen cheer.

Around the grass we went. I caught William's gaze out of the corner of my eye. He was on edge. This was too easy, too nice. Nothing with the Queen ever went this easy. And from the stains of blood on the grass, I did not expect things to end well. It didn't matter if the diamond—fake though it was—was in my pocket. She could just as easily loot it from my dead body as she could from my hand.

We were just nearing the seventh wicket when the queen pulled off her hat and dashed it to the ground. "I'm hot," she cursed then stomped the hat. Standing very close to her, I saw beads of sweat dripping down her forehead. They were tinted orange. She wiped the back of her hand across her forehead. When she saw her skin was marred with the red liquid, she huffed heavily. "We're done. I've won. Countess,

you're finished there. Off with their heads," she said, motioning toward the foreign visitors.

It took a moment for the Japanese guests to understand her words. The automatons and the Queen's guards closed in on them. They screamed and tried to flee, but it was too late.

"Bring their blood," the Countess said to her henchman, who nodded.

"Frances," the Queen called to the Countess. "Inside. Now. Bring the book."

The Countess nodded.

The Queen headed back inside. Her consort sat in his chair, barely aware that anything was happening. He simply smiled and gazed absently forward.

"I recognize him," William whispered as we followed behind the queen. "He's a Scottish Lord. He went missing about a year ago."

"A year ago?" I asked, remembering the box we'd delivered to the Queen via the *Medusa*.

"I guess they presumed him dead," William said.

"He might as well be," Jack said.

We followed the Queen of Hearts into the abbey. She led us to the room where we'd first met her. There, her long table was set out and had a number of instruments thereon.

The henchman entered the room behind us carrying a large copper bowl. Inside were the heads of three of the Japanese girls. Their blood pooled at the bottom of the basin.

"Get to work," the Queen told the Countess.

The Countess didn't look at us as she worked busily. She arranged objects, dried herbs, bits of bone, hair, and other oddities as she flipped through the book she'd brought with her. Seeing her manner was so easy, I began to wonder if I was misguided to place my trust in her. What if, after all, the Countess was in league with the Queen?

The Queen pulled off her thick scarf and unbuttoned her jacket. She stripped down to her corset. She was just a dainty thing, and she was undeniably beautiful. But more than that, she was dangerous.

"Bring Newell," she told her henchman. He disappeared down the hallway.

"Let's see it," the Queen said. She turned to me and opened her hand.

"First, your word that William's debt—and Jabberwocky's—is paid. None of us are indebted to you. Your word."

The Queen rolled her eyes. "A stickler for formality, Bandersnatch?"

"Afraid so. Mad times. Can't be sure of anything without a promise."

"Fine," the Queen said with a huff. "The debt is clear…if."

"If?"

"If this is the Koh-i-Noor. Tell me, Bandersnatch, how did you procure it?"

"All that matters is what we won, not how we worked."

"But that's the question, isn't it? I've had eyes on you and Caterpillar, and on that diamond, for days. We've seen you at the exhibition, but no one saw you lift the diamond. When did you take it?"

"Last night."

"How? No one saw you."

"I wouldn't be a very good thief if anyone saw me, now would I?"

At that, the Queen laughed.

A moment later, the henchman entered with a wiry-looking man who was wearing large round glasses and an oversized suit.

"Sit," she demanded shrilly. She set the diamond in front of him.

The man gasped.

I kept my gaze straight. I would show nothing.

"Is it the real diamond or not?" the Queen demanded.

"Where did you get this?" the man exclaimed. "How?"

"Shut your mouth. Now, tell the truth or I'll cut out your tongue. Is it the Koh-i-Noor or not?"

The man pulled a jeweler's monocle from his pocket and pressed it into his eye socket. He lifted the diamond and studied it closely.

I bit my tongue hard. If the lie was discovered, I would have to murder her right there. There was no other way out. I looked at the floor, hoping the Countess was as good at concealing what she knew. So far, she had not betrayed me. If she was planning to do so, now was the moment.

"Lifeless hunk of rock. Dull. Large. Not a shimmer to it," the man said then set the jewel aside.

The Queen turned on me, fury in her face.

She opened her mouth to speak when the gem master interjected. "Yes, this is most definitely the Koh-i-Noor."

A massive weight of relief washed over me.

"This dead looking stone?" the Queen asked sharply.

The man nodded. "It's a grand but lifeless thing."

The Queen turned and smiled at me. "Very good, Bandersnatch. Now, get him out of here," the Queen said then motioned for her henchman to take the gem master from the room.

"Prepare the potion, Countess," the Queen said then turned to me. "Why don't you stay? It will be very exciting to watch. And you've always struck me as someone with curious eyes."

"Watch?"

"Watch. Watch me be reborn."

22
THE MOCK PHOENIX

THE COUNTESS STOOD OVER THE table mixing items into a silver bowl. As she dropped each item therein, she intoned just under her breath. I'd known the Countess since I was a girl. I always admired her, called her friend. And I knew very well that her interest in the occult went beyond occasionally browsing her Uncle Horace's old books. I had always fashioned her more a tinker than a mage, but I could see how those lines could easily blend. She poured the blood from the bowl that contained the heads of the Japanese ladies, then added blood from two other vials.

A nauseous feeling swept over me. The smell of death and decay perfumed the air.

"Now, the diamond," the Countess said.

"Grab that mallet," the Queen instructed William.

William clenched his jaw together. Smothering his feelings, he picked up a wooden mallet that been sitting just beside the door.

The Queen set the faux kor-i-noor on the table. "Smash it."

"But it's a diamond," Jack interjected.

The Countess turn to William. "It is hard, but it will break. Put your back into it."

Frowning, William took aim. He lifted the mallet high then, with a hard swing, he brought down.

The table cracked under the pressure, the tabletop splintering. The Countess reached out to steady a candlestick before it fell over. In the concave of the table, the rock lay shattered into three large chunks. Diamond powder lay all around them.

The Countess took the mallet from William then smashed the rest into powder. When she was done, she collected all the powder and dropped it into the concoction.

She looked at the Queen. "I have made it as written here, but there is no saying it will work. At best, it will do as the Priest of Sekhmet has described in this writing. At worst, you may become very ill. This is not without risk. I have done everything I can. You cannot hold me accountable if something goes wrong."

The Queen narrowed her eyes at the Countess. "If it has been done properly, then we have nothing to worry about, Frances."

"And if the translation is off, or if the spell is a lie, you may become gravely ill, Anastasia," the Countess hissed.

The Queen glared hard at her. "Just say the words."

From her bag, the Countess pulled out a cloth on which had been decorated with Egyptian cartouche. She draped it around her neck. "Get back," she told us and the Queen's henchman.

We all moved toward the door.

A terrible feeling racked my stomach.

The Countess then began intoning in a language I did not recognize.

"The Goddess Sekhmet was a destroyer. She was a Goddess to be feared. We are all going to die," the Queen's henchman said.

"This is not how I thought this day was going to go," Jack said.

My stomach shook. The diamond was a fake, but the Countess's spell was real. What would happen now?

As the Countess spoke, the sky began to darken. In the distance, I heard the crack of lightning. Outside, the wind blew hard, and the clouds began rolling strangely. Everything went black. Twinkling lights shot across the sky. The small fire in the fireplace grew higher.

The Countess lifted a silver rod, and chanting some unknown words, she struck the rod on the side of the bowl.

The sharp sound followed by a strange vibration swept across the room. My hair stood on end.

"We need to go," Jack whispered.

The Countess lifted the rod once more and spoke again.

I looked at William who was staring with wide eyes. He turned to me. "If this works, if she takes on this power, what will happen? We need to stop the Countess," he said, then reached for his gun.

I shook my head. "No. Wait."

"Friends, we need to leave," Jack said again as he moved toward the door.

The Countess lowered the rod once more, knocking it on the side of the bowl.

Lightning cracked. The mixture inside the bowl began to swirl of its own accord.

"Yes," the Queen screamed. "Yes!"

The Countess lifted her rod a third time. The wind outside whipped hard. Thunder rolled and lightning cracked. The flame inside the fireplace burned wildly, the flames leaping out of the confines of the fireplace.

I heard the door behind us open. I looked back to see that Jack had left.

"Alice," William whispered. He had his pistol in hand. "We can't permit it."

"Wait," I said.

"Alice?"

"Do you trust me?"

He nodded. "With my life."

"Then wait."

The Countess dropped the rod a fourth time. The liquid in the bowl flared with bright purple light. Then, all at once, everything went silent.

Her hands shaking, the Countess poured the liquid from the silver bowl into a glass goblet which she then handed to the Queen. The liquid moved and sparkled, purple flame flickering at its surface.

"To eternal life," the Queen of Hearts said, lifting her chalice in a toast. Eyes closed, she drained the cup.

We waited.

At first, nothing happened.

The Queen opened her eyes and glared at the Countess. "It didn't work," she screeched. But before the Countess could respond, the Queen's body jerked. She dropped the crystal goblet. It fell to the floor, smashing into pieces.

She jerked again.

Orange light flashed through the Queen's body. It moved down her limbs, twisting like vines of fiery light just underneath the Queen's skin. Her hair broke free of its pins. Her long locks blew in a wild torrent around her. The Queen opened her eyes. I gasped to see they were alive with brimstone. Orange light shot from her fingertips. Everything in the room began to tremble.

"It worked," the Countess whispered, fear and awe in her voice. She stepped away from the Queen. "It worked." The Countess passed me a frightened and confused glance.

"I feel it. I am immortal," the Queen screamed.

"Alice," William said, reaching out to take my hand. "We need to leave."

It wasn't possible. The gem wasn't real. It shouldn't have worked.

The Countess grabbed her book and moved toward us.

The Queen laughed wildly. Surrounded by a halo of light, she began to rise off the ground. She floated at least a foot above the floor, her entire body alive with orange light.

And then, there was a strange rumble in the sky.

Lightning cracked.

A sharp wind blew, blowing open the windows. An awful smell perfumed the air. The scents of sulfur and rot rode on the breeze.

"Sekhmet," the henchman whispered.

A strange voice spoke on the wind. It echoed around the room. It was soft, female, and very angry.

"What is it? What is she sayi—" the Queen began, looking at the Countess.

But her words were cut off midspeech by a strange, sick laugh that echoed around the room.

The Queen's body froze in place, suspended in the air. The orange light died down, and we watched in horror as the veins under the Queen's skin began to grow black and pulse toward the surface. The glow in her eyes dimmed. They began to turn solid black.

The Queen tried to break free. "What's happening? What's happening?" she demanded of the Countess who backed toward the door.

Her face twisting, the Queen's mouth suddenly clamped shut. Her body twisted oddly and then we heard a terrible crunch, then another, as the Queen's body jerked from side to side like invisible hands were breaking her into pieces.

At last, she let out a terrible scream.

An invisible force slammed her to the wall, and then to another wall, over and over again. At the last moment, as the Queen hung in the air very still, that strange voice spoke once more.

The Countess gasped.

And then the Queen exploded.

"Alice," William shouted, pulling me close, shielding me. Blood and bits of the Queen of Hearts sprayed around the room.

The Countess yelped.

I looked in time to see the book she had been holding burst into flames. She dropped it on the floor. It disintegrated to ash.

When it was over, we looked back at the terrible sight. The Queen of Hearts had been shredded into pieces.

And at my feet lay her heart.

23
TODAY'S ALICE

THE COUNTESS'S AUTO PULLED UP to the door of The Mushroom. Wordlessly, Jack got out and went inside. None of us had said a word as we left the Queen's manor. We'd left unimpeded. The Queen's sycophants, glassy-eyed creatures such as they were, seemed to awake from a strange stupor. When we left, they were milling about as if they'd just awakened from a dream. And no one, not even her main henchman, had tried to stop us.

"Countess," I said carefully, setting my hand on hers. She was clutching the steering wheel so hard her knuckles had gone white.

The Countess turned and smiled softly at me. "If you need anything, Alice, please don't hesitate to call on me," she said then looked back at William. "I think things will be different from now on. Please know that

I'm here for you both."

I nodded. "Thank you."

"Lord Dodgson will be sorry to lose you," the Countess said.

"He'll recover."

She nodded knowingly then patted my hand once more.

William and I got out of the vehicle. With a wave, the Countess drove off.

"I feel like I'm waking up from a bad dream," William said.

I slipped my hand into his. "William, I owe you an apology."

He shook his head. "No, I owe you one."

We both chuckled.

"What if we simply move past the apologies? There is no use in going back to yesterday. Let's be today's Alice and William," he suggested.

"Starting from now, though. And after a bath," I said, looking down at my clothes which were still splattered with goo.

William laughed. "Of course," he said then cast a glance back at the pub. "I need to talk to Jack."

I nodded. "You know where to find me."

William pulled me close and set his forehead against mine. "I love you, Alice."

"I love you too."

With that, he turned and headed inside.

24
FALLING STARS

THE MOMENT I ENTERED OUR flat, Bess let out an excited squeal. "Alice," she yelled excitedly. She turned to embrace me but stopped. "What in creation are you covered in? Ew!"

"You don't want to know. And I need to change. Immediately. But what happened?"

"Henry just left. He's having a carriage brought around. Alice, he proposed!"

She stuck out her hand. On her finger was a beautiful ring with pearls set in a flower design around a sparkling center gem—a diamond, but not quite a diamond. "Isn't it beautiful?"

"A new beginning. How very exciting," I exclaimed.

Bess hugged her hand to her heart. "It's been a very odd day. Just out of the blue, he asked me to marry him. Can you believe it? And the weather. Have you noticed? It was so strange today. Thunder. Lightning. Some sort of odd eclipse. There were falling stars in the middle of the day."

"A good sign, perhaps?"

Bess smiled, squinting her eyes closed. Her face was radiant. She turned and looked at me. "Oh, Alice! You look just awful. Get that off at once. But what's this expression on your face? You look so...so, I don't know what!"

"Relieved? Elated? Happy?"

"Why? What's happened?"

"William."

Bess squealed. "What a wonderful day."

Dinah, who was observing us both from her perch on the window seal, meowed at us.

Bess laughed. "You see, even Dinah agrees. And what about you, Chess?" Bess asked, turning to my clockwork cat.

From his position on my cot, the Cheshire cat flashed us a toothy smile.

We both laughed.

"Now, get cleaned up. We're going on a picnic. Oh, Alice, why do I get the feeling that everything will be different now?"

"Because it will."

Bess signed happily. "A wonderland of opportunity awaits us."

"Indeed. How very curious."

25
EPILOGUE

"YOUR MOVE," WILLIAM SAID.

I picked a pawn and moved him across the chest board. "Check."

"You think you're so clever," William replied, moving his king.

"Don't you?"

"Don't I what?"

"Think I'm clever."

"Of course I do. Stop trying to distract me."

"Me?" I asked, tilting my head sideways and looking him over, my eyes radiating desire.

"Oh, now you're really playing," William said. He slipped out of his seat and onto the loveseat beside me. He moved my hair aside and kissed my neck.

"Now who is playing?" I whispered.

"After a look like that, how can I resist?"

The grandfather clock struck six. The last chime had just sounded when I heard a knock on the front door of the guesthouse.

"Henry and Bess?" William asked.

I nodded. "They returned from Bath today."

William kissed me on the forehead. "No wonder Maggie has been cooking all day. I thought perhaps the Countess had returned."

I shook my head. "I had a letter from her this morning. She's still abroad." In fact, the situation with the Queen had rattled the Countess in a way I didn't understand. She'd been quiet and thoughtful. Despite her peculiar reaction, she'd still done everything she could to help us. She'd situated Henry into a shop in Twickenham and paid for Bess's and Henry's wedding. William and I, who were more wed in spirit, had taken up residence in the guesthouse at Strawberry Hill. The Countess, quite rightly, suspected that I would be able to make something of the old printing press that had sat cobwebbed since her uncle's death.

"I'll go welcome them. Why don't you show Bess what you've been working on?" William said, motioning to the stack of papers I had sitting on my desk.

I nodded, kissed him quickly, and then rose. William exited the room, closing the wood panel doors behind him.

On my desk near the fireplace, I had a stack of papers. Notes, illustrations, and outlines covered the pages. I picked up my writing tablet. I was just about finished. I smiled when I thought of Bess's reaction to my news.

"*Wonderland* by Alice Lewis. Subtitled, *Imaginative Tales for Children.* How does that sound, Chess?" I asked, turning to my clockwork cat. The little creature, who'd been grooming his paw, looked up at me and blinked his wide, aquamarine-colored eyes.

I laughed then kicked a ball of yarn toward him. Excited, he crouched, his gears clicking, then pounced.

Grinning, I looked at my reflection in the mirror over the fireplace. I pushed my hair behind my ears and straightened the black headband I was

wearing. In the mirror, I saw the reflection of the yard outside. The lights inside Strawberry Hill House glimmered through the windows. But then I noticed something odd. A hooded figure carrying a lamp moved toward the castle. I turned and looked out the window. It was dusk, but not yet entirely dark. I peered through the window. No one was there.

I looked back at the mirror once more. This time, to my surprise— given it was autumn—the mirror reflected a wintery scene outside my window. The grounds were completely covered in snow, squalls of white whipping across the landscape. And at the center of the grounds, I saw a woman dressed in all white. She carried a lantern and wore a crown of ice on her head.

Gasping, I turned around and looked out the window once more. Again, no one was there. The leaves were hued sunset orange, ruby red, and gold in color. They swayed in the breeze, shimmering softly in the dying sunlight.

"Alice?" William called.

I looked down at my manuscript. *Imaginative Tales* indeed. The first tale in my collection was none other than the tale of the Snow Queen. I grinned. Strawberry Hill was certainly an odd little castle, built by the Countess's odd uncle, and filled with odd fixtures, like the odd mirror above my fireplace. As it turned out, it was the perfect place for an odd girl like me.

"Coming," I called, casting a glance once more at the mirror. This time, it showed only its true reflection.

Surely, I was dreaming.

But the question is, can a person dream while she is awake?

Perhaps, if she has the right looking glass.

ABOUT THE AUTHOR

Melanie Karsak is the NY Times bestselling author of *The Airship Racing Chronicles*, *The Harvesting Series*, and *The Celtic Blood Series*. A steampunk connoisseur, zombie whisperer, and heir to the iron throne, the author currently lives in Florida with her husband and two children. She is an Instructor of English at Eastern Florida State College.

Keep in touch with the author online.

www.melaniekarsak.com
www.facebook.com/AuthorMelanieKarsak
ww.twitter.com/melaniekarsak
www.pinterest.com/melaniekarsak

FIND MY BOOKS ON AMAZON.COM

Made in the USA
Columbia, SC
29 July 2022

64050499R00138